The Missing Kitten

and other tales

The Missing Kitten

and other tales

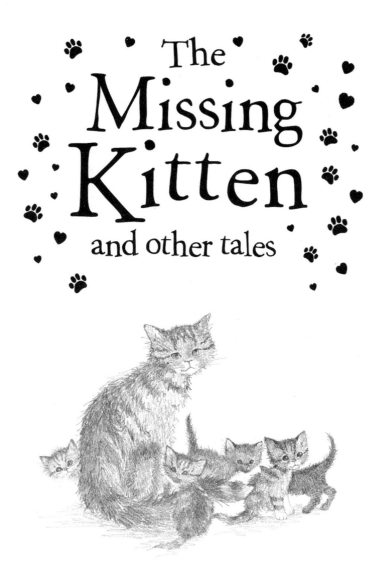

by Holly Webb

Illustrated by Sophy Williams

tiger tales

tiger tales

5 River Road, Suite 128, Wilton, CT 06897
Published in the United States 2018
Text copyright © Holly Webb
The Missing Kitten originally published in 2013
The Unwanted Kitten originally published as
Sky the Unwanted Kitten 2008
The Abandoned Kitten originally published as
Misty the Abandoned Kitten 2010
Illustrations copyright © Sophy Williams
The Missing Kitten originally published in 2013
The Unwanted Kitten originally published as
Sky the Unwanted Kitten 2008
The Abandoned Kitten originally published as
Misty the Abandoned Kitten 2010
ISBN-13: 978-1-68010-415-8
ISBN-10: 1-68010-415-2
Printed in China
STP/1000/0138/0417
10 9 8 7 6 5 4 3 2 1

For more insight and activities, visit us at www.tigertalesbooks.com

.

Contents

The Missing Kitten

Contents

For Emily and the gorgeous Rosie Bumble

Chapter One
A Fresh Start

Suzanne looked around her new bedroom with delight. It was huge! And as it was up in the roof of the cottage, it was a really interesting shape, all ups and downs. There was a beautiful window as well, with a curly handle to open it, and a big, wide windowsill she could sit on. Her old bedroom had been tiny, and a very boring, square shape.

"Good, isn't it?" Jackson, her big brother, poked his head around the door. He had the bedroom next to hers, which was basically the other half of the roof space. Mom and Dad had said that their bedrooms used to be the attic.

"I love it," Suzanne said happily. "The window's the best thing! I love seeing all the fields and trees, and look! Cows! Out my bedroom window!"

Jackson chuckled. "Cows, not cars. Now *that's* a change! Yeah, it's really good. Except everything's pretty far away."

Suzanne nodded slowly. "There is a store in the town," she reminded him.

Jackson made a face. "Yeah, one store! And a blacksmith. How weird is that?"

"And the school's in the town, too," Suzanne added, very quietly. "I wish we didn't have to change schools." That was the thing she was least happy about with their move to the countryside. She was really going to miss her old school, and her friends. Lucy and Ella had said they'd come and stay over the next vacation, but that was a long time away. And meanwhile, she was going to start at a school where she didn't know anyone, and she certainly didn't have any friends.

"It'll be all right," Jackson told her cheerfully, and Suzanne sighed. He wasn't worried. He never was. Jackson was really sporty, and he found it very easy to make friends. And yet he didn't show off, so people just wanted to hang

13

out with him. Suzanne wished she knew how he did it.

"Did you hear that rustling noise?" Jackson pointed up at the ceiling. "I bet there are mice in all that thatch. Remember to tell Mom and Dad about that, Suzanne. You need to start working on them again about a kitten, now that we're here. They said maybe after we'd moved, didn't they?"

Suzanne grinned at him. "I know! I thought I'd maybe give them a day, though, before I started asking. Let them get some boxes unpacked first...." She looked up, too. "Do you really think there are mice?"

Jackson gazed thoughtfully at the ceiling. "Probably. It sounds like it to me. Unless it's a rat, of course."

"Ugh! Okay, I'll ask Mom now. No way am I living in a house with a rat!" Suzanne shuddered.

"I'm with you on that," Jackson grinned. "Rats can be pretty big, you know. Bigger than a kitten, anyway." He made a rat-like face, pulling his lips back to show his teeth.

"Stop it!" Suzanne cried. "Maybe we can get a grown-up cat then. I don't mind if it isn't a kitten. I'd just love to have any kind of cat and they did say maybe we could. You'll help, won't you? You'll ask, too?"

Jackson nodded. "Yeah. Although I don't like the idea of coming down in the morning to find a row of dead mice on the doormat. That's what Sam says his cat does."

Suzanne looked worried. "I think I'd rather have a cat that just scares the mice away…."

Suzanne started her kitten campaign while everyone was sitting down eating lunch. It felt really odd seeing their old table in a completely different kitchen.

"It's so quiet," Mom said happily, looking out the open window. "I don't think I've heard a single car since we got here. I love that we're down at the end of the road."

"I keep thinking there's something missing," Dad admitted. "But it'll be great once we're used to it. And the air smells amazing."

Jackson sniffed loudly. "That's the cows, Dad."

Suzanne made a face at him. She didn't want him distracting Mom and Dad—this was a great opportunity to mention a kitten. She took a deep breath. "It's not a bit like Edward Street, is it?" she said, thinking about their old home. "With all the traffic...." She swallowed, and glanced hopefully from Mom to Dad and back again. "You wouldn't worry about a cat getting run over here, would you?"

Dad snorted with laughter and turned to Mom. "You win, Laura. She lasted more than an hour."

Suzanne blinked. "What do you mean?"

Mom reached out an arm and hugged her around the shoulder. "Dad and I were talking about it last night, Suzanne. We wondered how long you'd be able to wait before you asked about a cat. I said that I thought it would be once we'd settled in a bit, and Dad said you'd ask the moment we got here. So I won, and now he has to cook dinner tonight!"

"Simple. Take-out pizza," Dad said, taking a huge bite of sandwich.

Mom smiled at him. "You do realize it's a 20-minute drive to the nearest store, now, don't you?"

"You mean you were just waiting for me to ask? So, can we have one?" Suzanne said hopefully, eager to get back to talking about kittens.

Mom nodded slowly. "Yes. But we can't go off to an animal shelter tomorrow—we need to do some unpacking, and besides, I don't have a clue where the closest one is."

"I could find out!" Suzanne said eagerly. "It's just—it would be really nice to have time to get to know the kitten before school starts. We only have two weeks, and then Jackson and I won't be home for most of the day."

Dad nodded. "I know, Suzanne, but

19

I don't think we'll be able to find you a kitten right now. I know it would be wonderful to have one while you're still at home. But it won't be a huge problem if you're at school. Mom'll be at work, but I'll be at home, so the kitten won't be lonely. And your new school's really close. You'll be home in 10 minutes."

Suzanne nodded. That was another thing that was different, being able to walk to school. Mom and Dad had even said she and Jackson could walk by themselves, if they wanted, since there were sidewalks the entire way.

"I suppose." Suzanne nodded. "So, we can really have a cat? You actually mean it? We can look for one?"

"Promise," Dad told her solemnly.

Suzanne beamed at him. She could come home from school and play with her cat. Her own cat! She'd wanted to have one for so long, and now it was going to happen.

"Suzanne! I'm off to town," Dad yelled up the stairs.

Suzanne shoved an armful of T-shirts into the drawer and dashed out of her room. "I'm coming!"

She really wanted to walk there. They'd seen the town a couple of times before. The first time was when they came to look at the house. Mom had gotten her new job at the hospital, and Mom and Dad explained that they

21

would need to move, since it was too far for Mom to drive every day. Suzanne had really missed her for those few weeks when she'd been leaving early and not getting back until it was almost time for Suzanne to go to bed. Now that they'd moved, the hospital was only half an hour away, in Longwood, the nearest big town to their tiny little town, which was called Longwood Hills. Once they'd made the decision that Mom would take the job, and agreed to buy the cottage, Suzanne and Jackson had gone for a day's visit at their new school and seen the small town again. But Suzanne had been so nervous about the school that she couldn't remember what it was like.

"It's so pretty," she said, as they

walked along the sidewalk. "Look at all the flowers. I saw a rabbit last night, Dad, did I tell you?"

"Only about six times! I almost had a heart attack when you screamed like that. I thought you'd fallen out the window."

"Sorry! I was excited! I've never seen a rabbit in my yard before!" Suzanne giggled. "Can we go down here? Is it the right way?"

Dad nodded. "Yup, this is the quickest path down to the town, the way you and Jackson will go to school, probably."

Suzanne swallowed nervously. She was still worrying about the school. It was tiny, which was nice, she supposed. There wouldn't be that many people to get to know. But they'd probably all been together since preschool. They might not want a stranger joining their class at all.

Dad nudged her gently with his elbow. "You had a good time on your visit, didn't you?"

Suzanne looked up at him, surprised.

"It was pretty obvious what you were thinking, sweetheart."

"I suppose. Yes. Everyone was nice. But that was just one morning. I have to go there every day…."

"It'll be great. You'll be fine, I'm sure you will."

Suzanne nodded. She didn't really want to think about it. "Look—is that the town? I can see houses." She ran on ahead. "And there's the store, Dad, look."

"I'd better find the list," Dad muttered, searching his pockets. "We definitely need bread. Can you be in charge of finding that for me? Now where on earth did I put that list?"

But Suzanne wasn't listening. She had seen something—a bulletin board in the store window. It was full of advertisements—exercise classes in the church hall, someone offering to make celebration cakes, an almost-new lawnmower for sale....

And a litter of kittens, three black-and-white, one tabby, ready to leave their mother now, free to good homes.

Chapter Two
Meeting the Kittens

"Dad! Look!" Suzanne was so excited, she couldn't stand still—she was dancing from foot to foot, pointing madly at the flier.

"What?" Her dad hurried up, peering into the window. "Oh! I can see why you're so excited. 'Ready now,' hmmm?" He read the flier thoughtfully, and then took out his phone.

"Are you going to call them?" Suzanne squeaked excitedly.

"No. I'm going to put the number into my phone, get some bread and milk, and go home and talk it over with your mother. Can you imagine what she'd say if we went out for groceries and came home with a kitten?"

Suzanne sighed. "I guess you're right. It would be funny though." She giggled. "'Hi, Mom, here's the milk....' And we take a kitten out of the bag!"

"It might have been here a while, this flier," Dad pointed out. "The kittens might already be gone. Don't get your hopes up, okay?"

Suzanne nodded. But as they paid for the groceries, she took a deep breath and smiled at the lady behind the

27

counter. She hated talking to people she didn't know, but this was important. "Excuse me, but do you see the flier in the window about the kittens? Has it been up for long—I mean, do you know if there are any left?"

The lady beamed at her. "You'd like a kitten, hmm? Julie Mallins will be happy. She only put the flier up earlier this week, and I know she's still looking for homes for all of them."

"Really?" Suzanne was dancing around again. She just couldn't help it. "Oh, Dad, can we go home and talk to Mom about it now, please?"

"All right, all right!" Dad grinned, raising his eyebrows at the lady.

Suzanne ran all the way home—in fact, she went twice as far as Dad did, because he wouldn't run, so she kept having to turn around and run all the way back to him to tell him to hurry up. When she raced in through the front door of the cottage, she was completely out of breath.

"Mom! Mom!" she gasped, running from the living room to the kitchen and back to the bottom of the stairs.

"What's the matter, sweetheart?" Her mom backed out of the cupboard under the stairs, where she'd been putting coats and boots away.

"Mom, there's someone in town who has a litter of kittens that they want to give away!"

"Really?"

"There was a flier up in the town store." Dad came in, holding out his phone. "I have the number. What do you think?"

Suzanne bit her lip to keep herself from shrieking "Please, please, please." Her mom was very firm about not whining, and she really didn't want to get on her mom's bad side right now.

"Well, I suppose we could ask to go and look at them...," her mom said, rather doubtfully. "I'm just a little worried because the house is all upside down right now while we're still unpacking. Wouldn't that be stressful for a kitten?"

Suzanne's face fell. Mom was right. "Maybe we could wait?" Suzanne whispered. "Maybe we could just choose a kitten and ask them to keep it for us a little longer?" She really wanted to have a kitten now, but she didn't want their new pet to start out scared by all the boxes everywhere.

Dad hugged her. "Well, let's see what Julie says—she's the owner," he explained to Mom. "She might not think it's a problem. To be honest, we've done most of the unpacking in the kitchen already. We could keep the kitten in there for the time being—I think you have to keep new kittens in one room to start off with, anyway."

Mom nodded. "I'd forgotten that. We used to have a cat when I was little," she told Suzanne, "but that was such a long time ago. We'll all have to learn how to take care of a cat together."

"What?" Jackson put his head around the kitchen door. "Are we getting one? What's happening?"

"Suzanne found a flier about a litter of kittens needing homes," Dad told him. "We should have known—if there were kittens around, Suzanne was bound to find them! Should I call this lady, then?"

Mom nodded, and Suzanne flung her arms around her. She held her breath and listened as Dad made the phone call.

32

"Hi, is this Julie? We saw your flier about the kittens.... Mmm.... We wondered if we'd be able to come and see them. Uh-huh. Well, now's great, if that's really okay with you. Fantastic. Spruce Street. Oh, off the main road? See you in about 10 minutes, then."

Suzanne gasped. Ten minutes! Ten minutes until they saw their kitten!

"Here they are."

Julie turned out to be a really sweet lady who'd adopted Goldie, the kittens' mom, after finding her eating scraps of bread under her bird feeder because she was a stray, and so terribly hungry.

"It took weeks to even get her to

come inside," Julie told Suzanne, as she led them through to the kitchen. "But she's settling down now. I think she knew she needed to let someone take care of her, so she could have her kittens somewhere nice and warm."

"How old are the kittens?" Suzanne's mom asked as Julie opened the kitchen door.

"Ten weeks—the vet said they should be fine to go to new homes," Suzanne heard Julie say. But she wasn't really concentrating. Instead, she was staring at the basket in the corner, where a beautiful brownish tabby cat was curled up, with four kittens piled around and on top of her.

"Goodness, she looks tired," Mom said.

"Yes, I think she is, poor thing. She's been a really good mom, but she was so thin to start with, aside from her huge tummy full of kittens. I was worried that she wouldn't be able to feed them, but she's done very well. They're all practically weaned now—they love their food!"

Woken by the voices, one of the kittens popped his head up, his big orange ears twitching with interest.

"Oh, look at him!" Suzanne whispered. "His ears are too big for him!"

Julie nodded. "I know, he's cute, isn't he? He has big paws, too; I think he's going to be a really big cat."

The kitten gently nudged the brother or sister next to him with the side of his chin, and the rest of the kittens popped up in a line, staring at Suzanne and Jackson.

The other three were black-and-white, very pretty, without the massive ears. They had enormous whiskers instead—great big white mustaches.

"I like the orange one," Jackson said. "That one's a boy, right?"

Julie nodded. "Yes, and the three black-and-white ones are girls."

"I like him, too," Suzanne agreed. "Will they let us pet them? Is that okay?"

"They're usually very friendly. Especially Ginger."

"Oh, is that his name?" Suzanne tried

not to sound disappointed. She would have liked to choose a name together for their kitten—Ginger was what all orange cats were called!

"Oh, no. I've tried not to give them names—I'm hoping to find homes for them all, and if I name them I'll just want to keep them. But it's hard not to think of him as Ginger."

The orange kitten was standing up now, arching his back and stretching as he climbed out of the basket. He looked sideways at Suzanne with his big blue eyes to check that she was admiring how handsome he was as he stretched. She was watching him eagerly, and she gave a little sigh of delight as he stepped toward her, gently rubbing himself against her arm.

"Oh, he has boots!" Suzanne looked over at Jackson and her mom and dad. "Look, he has furry white boots on!"

Mom laughed. "He does look like he has boots on," she agreed. "Those are very cute."

"I know lots of cats have white paws, but I've never seen one where the white goes that far up before." Suzanne petted the tabby kitten lovingly, and his black-and-white sisters followed him out of the basket, looking for some attention, too. Their mother stared watchfully after them, and then seemed to decide that Suzanne and the others weren't dangerous to her babies. She gave a massive yawn, and curled up for a nap.

The girl kittens let Suzanne's mom and dad pet them, then they took off chasing after a feathery cat toy, racing around the kitchen and batting it ahead of them with their paws. The orange kitten watched them, but he didn't join in. Instead, he placed a hopeful paw on Suzanne's knee, and she looked back at him, just as hopefully. Did he want to be picked up?

"He's very cuddly," Julie said quietly. "He's a real people cat. Try and put him on your lap."

Suzanne gently wrapped her hands around his fluffy middle. Even though he was the biggest of the kittens, he still

39

felt tiny—so light, as though there was nothing to him.

The kitten gave a pleased little squeak, and padded his fat white paws up and down her jeans as though he were testing how comfy she was. Suzanne found herself smoothing her jeans, wanting him to think she was nice to sit on. He padded all the way around in a circle a couple of times, and then wobbled and flopped down, stretching his front paws out, and flexing his claws gently in and out of the denim fabric of her jeans.

"That tickles!" Suzanne giggled, petting him under his little white chin.

The kitten purred delightedly. That was the best place, the spot he was always itchy. He pointed his chin to the ceiling and purred louder, telling her to keep going.

Jackson joined in, running one finger gently down the kitten's back. "His fur's really soft. And look at his paws! They're bright pink underneath!" The kitten was enjoying the petting so much that he'd collapsed into a happy heap on his side, purring like a motorboat.

Suzanne looked down at his paws and laughed—they really were pink. A sort of pinkish-apricot color, and so soft and smooth-looking.

"They'll probably get darker once he starts going outside," Julie explained. "They've only been indoors so far. He'd need to stay in for a little longer if you decide to take him." She looked at Suzanne's mom and dad.

Suzanne and Jackson got up, then both turned to look at them, too, and their mom laughed. She turned to Julie and asked hopefully, "I don't suppose you could give us some cat litter, could you? The store in town would have cat food...."

"You mean we can take him now?" Suzanne gasped.

Her mom shrugged and smiled. "Why not?"

Chapter Three
A Scary First Day

"Dad, we're almost out of Boots's food. There's only the salmon flavor left, and I don't think he liked that one very much."

Boots wrapped himself lovingly around Suzanne's legs. He knew very well what was in those cans, and he didn't see any reason why he shouldn't have a second breakfast.

Calling him Boots had been Jackson's idea. Suzanne had suggested Sam, but it was like Ginger—a little bit too ordinary for such a special cat. Boots was much better.

Jackson looked up from his huge pile of toast. "We could go to the store," he said. "I've almost finished the bread, and there's not a lot for lunch."

"I've got a work call in a few minutes," said Dad. He looked at them thoughtfully. "Though I suppose you two could go, if you'd like."

"On our own?" Suzanne stared at him.

"Why not? You were going to try it when school started next week, weren't you? Just be careful, and stick together."

Suzanne shut her eyes for a second at

44

the mention of school. She was trying not to think about it. "Will you take care of Boots while we're out?" she said seriously.

"Suzanne! You'll only be gone half an hour!" Dad grinned.

"But he's not used to me not being here!" It was true. Suzanne had spent all of her time with Boots since they'd brought him home, only leaving him at night, when he was safely tucked in his cardboard box, on an old towel, and next to a hot water bottle to feel like his mother and the other kittens. Just until he got used to them not being next to him.

"I think it would be good for him to see you go out," her dad said gently. "I know you don't want to think about school, Suzanne, but you do go on Monday. Boots has had a whole week of you around all the time. He needs to learn to be without you."

"But he'll be lonely," Suzanne said worriedly.

"It's only for half an hour," Dad reminded her.

"When we're back at school it won't be!"

"Then he'll have me for company while I'm working. And you know how he loves the computer."

Suzanne smiled. It was true. Boots was fascinated by Dad's computer. He seemed to love the way the keys went up and down. He would sit watching Dad type forever, just occasionally putting out a paw to try and join in. Then he

46

would look annoyed when Dad told him no. Secretly Suzanne was planning to let him try one day when she was using the laptop that she shared with Jackson. She wanted to see what Boots would write— she knew it would probably be a string of random letters, but she was hoping for a secret message!

"Come on, then." Jackson stuffed the last of the toast into his mouth. "Can we get some chips when we're at the store, Dad?"

"Sure. Here." Dad gave Jackson some money. "But I do want change. Be back by ten thirty, all right? I don't want to be pacing up and down outside looking for you."

"Are you really worried about school?" Jackson asked Suzanne as they wandered down the sidewalk in the direction of the town.

"A little." Suzanne sighed. "What if nobody talks to me?"

"Why wouldn't they?" Jackson asked, shrugging.

Suzanne shook her head. He was trying to be nice, but he just didn't get it.

"You had lots of friends at your old school," said Jackson. "Why do you think you won't make friends here?"

"It's such a little school," Suzanne tried to explain. "Only one class in each grade, and not that many kids in each class, either. They'll all know each other so well. Like I know Lucy and Ella." She wished she were as confident as Jackson.

He'd already managed to go out for a walk and found a couple of boys playing football. He'd joined in, and then he'd gone back to their house. Suzanne wasn't sure how he did it.

Jackson rolled his eyes. "Come on. We're almost there."

They went into the store, and Jackson went to look at football magazines, while Suzanne found the cat food. Then she realized that there were a couple of other girls standing behind her.

"Who's she?" one of them whispered.

"Don't you remember? It's that new girl. The one who came to school for a morning."

"Ohhh! What's her name?"

"Something weird. Amber or something."

Suzanne felt like her stomach was squeezing into a tiny knot inside her. She was the one they were talking about. The girl with the weird name. She wanted to scream, "Suzanne!" But she didn't. She grabbed a couple of cans of cat food, and scooted over to where Jackson was.

School was going to be a disaster. It was so obvious.

Suzanne lay in bed, watching her clock creep closer to seven. She'd been awake for a while, worrying about their first day at school, and now she just wished it would hurry up and be time.

A throaty purr distracted her, and a soft paw patted her chin. Boots liked her to be paying attention to him, not the clock.

"I'm glad I went downstairs and got you before breakfast," Suzanne said, tickling him behind the ears. "I know I look miserable, but you're making me feel a lot better."

Boots closed his eyes happily and purred even louder. Suzanne knew all the places he liked to be petted, and how he particularly liked being on her bed. It was much cozier than his basket.

"I'm really going to miss you today," Suzanne murmured. "I hope you'll be okay. Dad will take care of you." She sighed, a huge sigh that lifted up the comforter around her middle, and Boots's ears twitched excitedly. He wriggled forward, and peered down under the comforter. It was like a dark little nest, and he wriggled into it, just his tail sticking out, and flicking from side to side.

"What are you doing?" Suzanne giggled. "Silly cat! Oh, Boots, you're tickling my legs!"

Even the tail had disappeared now. Boots was a plump little mound traveling around under the comforter. Then he popped out at the other end of the bed, his orange fur looking all spiky and ruffled up. He shook himself and ran a paw over his ears.

Suzanne twitched her toes under the comforter, and he stopped washing and pounced on them excitedly, jumping from side to side as she wriggled them.

"You're awake!" Mom poked her head around the door. "Time to get up, Suzanne. Hello, Boots." She came in and patted him. "Are you worried that he'll miss you while you're at school?"

Suzanne nodded, and Mom hugged her. "It'll be fine, sweetheart. Now that he's allowed in the yard, he'll probably just go out and try to chase butterflies again." She looked at Suzanne. "And you'll be fine, too. Honestly. Try not to worry about it."

Suzanne nodded. But she wished she felt as sure as everybody else seemed to.

Boots sat on the back doorstep, next to his cat flap, staring around the yard. He was confused, and a little bored. Suzanne had gone somewhere. He'd known that she was going—she had picked him up and made a huge fuss over him before she went, and her voice had been different than normal, as though something were wrong. But he hadn't expected her to be gone this long.

He stalked crossly around the yard, sniffing at the grass, looking for something interesting to do. He sharpened his claws on the trunk of the apple tree, and tried to climb it, but he wasn't all that good at climbing yet, and he only got halfway up before he got worried and jumped down again. Then he had to sit and wash himself for a while, pretending that he'd never meant to climb it in the first place.

55

Where was she? Jackson was gone, too—he preferred to play with Suzanne, but Jackson was very good at inventing games with sticks, and pieces of string to chase.

Why had they gone away and left him? And when were they coming back?

Chapter Four
A Sneaky Follower

"Boots! Did you miss me?" Suzanne picked him up, and hugged him lovingly, and Boots rubbed his head against her cheek.

Dad had come to meet them from school, as it was the first day, but tomorrow they were going to walk there and back by themselves.

"Come and have a cookie," Dad

suggested. "Then you can both tell me what it was like, now that there's no one else around." When he'd asked Suzanne at the school gate how her day was, she'd just muttered, "Fine," but he could tell she was only being polite.

"It was all right." Jackson shrugged, munching a chocolate cookie. "Played football at lunch. The teacher was a little strict. Shouted at people for talking. But it was fine."

Dad looked over at Suzanne, who sighed. "It was okay. This girl named Izzie was told to show me around, and she was nice. She took me with her at recess and lunchtime. But—well, it was only because she had to."

"She might really like you!" Dad pointed out.

Suzanne ran one of Boots's huge ears between her fingers, and sighed. "Maybe…. It wasn't as bad as it could have been," she admitted. The two girls she'd seen in the store hadn't said anything else about her weird name, which was what she'd been worrying about. They'd been at the same table as Izzie and her at lunch, and they'd been friendly, and asked her where she lived, and if she took the bus to school.

59

It turned out that lots of the students did—they came from several different towns, and a school bus went around and picked them all up.

"It's nice that we can walk to school," she said to Dad, who was still looking worried about her.

Boots rubbed himself against her red sweater, leaving orange hairs all over it, and Suzanne petted him again. Whatever happened at school, at least she could come home and play with him. She couldn't imagine being without him now.

"You're sure you wouldn't like me to come with you?" Dad asked for about the fourth time.

"No!" Jackson said. "Honestly, Dad. We're fine. It takes about 10 minutes to get to school, and we don't even have to cross a road. Stop worrying."

Boots was sitting on the bottom step of the stairs, watching disapprovingly as Suzanne and Jackson got ready. They were going again, just like yesterday! Why was he being left behind? He let out a tiny, furious meow, but Suzanne only kissed the top of his head, and went out the door, leaving him with Dad.

Dad picked Boots up, and tickled his ears, before rubbing the top of his head. But then he put him back down on the stairs, and headed into the room where his computer was. He was going to be too busy to play, again.

61

Boots stalked into the kitchen and inspected his food bowl, which was empty. He had a little water, and looked at his basket. He didn't really feel like sleeping. And if this were anything like yesterday, Suzanne and Jackson would be gone for hours.

He didn't see why he couldn't go with them. Until yesterday, he'd been with Suzanne almost all the time.

Boots walked over to the cat flap and sniffed at it, carefully. They hadn't been gone long. Maybe, if he was quick, he could follow them. Boots shot out of the cat flap and dashed into the back yard. Suzanne and Jackson had gone out the front door, so he hurried around the side of the house, and on to the front yard. He nosed his way under the blue gate, flattening himself underneath the wooden panels, and coming out into the road, next to the car. His whiskers twitched excitedly as he tried to figure out which way Suzanne had gone. He could follow her scent, he was sure. He sniffed busily at the grass, and then set off running.

Suzanne and Jackson were halfway to school, walking down the sidewalk along the side of the big field, when suddenly, she stopped.

"Can you hear a meow?" Suzanne asked, and Jackson turned around to stare at her.

"Don't be silly. Come on!"

"No, I can hear meowing. I really can. It's Boots, I'm sure." Suzanne peered along the sidewalk behind them and laughed. "It is! Look!"

Boots was running after them, meowing happily, and as Suzanne crouched down to say hello, he clambered up into her lap and sat there, purring wearily. He'd had to run faster than ever before to catch up.

"What's he doing here?" Jackson shook his head. "Yes, you're very clever, Boots," he admitted, running one hand down the little kitten's back. "But now we have to take you back home, and we're going to be late."

"Do we have to take him back?" Suzanne asked sadly.

Jackson rolled his eyes. "Yes, of course we do! We can't take a cat to school, Suzanne!"

"I suppose not."

"And we have to run, because we're going to be late."

Suzanne swallowed anxiously. She didn't want to be late, to have to go in after everyone else, and explain what had happened. They hurried back down the sidewalk and across the street before bursting through the front door.

Dad came out of his office, looking worried. "What's the matter? Why are you back? I knew I should have gone with you!"

"Don't worry, Dad. Everything's fine." Suzanne held out her arms, full of purring tabby kitten. "Boots just followed us. He caught up with us as we were going past the big field. We had to bring him back." She put Boots into Dad's arms, and he stopped purring and glared at her. He'd gone to find her, and brought her back, and now she was going again!

"Sorry, Boots. I'd much rather stay with you." Suzanne petted his head as she turned to leave.

"Come on, Suzanne!" Jackson yelled from the door.

"You'd better run, sweetheart," Dad said. "I'd drive you, but driving would take longer than walking the short cut. I'll call the school and explain why you'll be a little late, don't worry."

"Thanks, Dad," said Suzanne.

When Suzanne and Jackson hurried onto the playground, the principal, Miss Wilson, was standing at the main door watching for them.

Suzanne was worried. Luckily, Miss Wilson didn't look angry. She just smiled at them as they raced toward her, and patted Jackson's shoulder. "Don't worry. I used to have a dog that followed me to school. Still, I've never heard of a cat doing it. He must be very fond of you."

Suzanne nodded proudly. She hadn't really thought of it like that.

"I explained to your teachers what happened, so just slip quietly into your classes, all right?"

"Thanks, Miss Wilson." Suzanne crept, mouse-like, along the hallway. It was all very well to say to slip in quietly, but everyone was still going to turn and stare at her. She eased open the door of her classroom, wincing as it creaked.

But her teacher, Mrs. Mason, just smiled at her and waved her over to her table, and went on pointing out something on the whiteboard.

"I wondered where you were!" Izzie whispered to her. "I thought you might not be coming back!"

"It wasn't that bad yesterday," Suzanne muttered.

"Are you okay?" said Izzie. "Did you

69

oversleep?"

Suzanne shook her head. "No. It sounds really silly, but I had to take my kitten home. He followed us to school."

"Your kitten did?" Izzie stared at her. "I didn't know you had a kitten! I've got a cat. His name is Oscar. But he's never followed me anywhere! He's too lazy. What's your kitten's name?"

"Boots." Suzanne smiled proudly. "We've only had him two weeks, and he isn't used to us leaving him. Mrs. Mason's giving us a look. I'll tell you more at recess, okay?"

Izzie grinned. "You're so lucky to have a kitten."

Suzanne nodded and stared at the whiteboard. Izzie was right, she realized. She really was lucky.

Chapter Five
Looking for Suzanne

"I'll keep Boots inside until after you've left," Dad said at breakfast the following morning. "If I don't open the cat flap for an hour or so, and I give him a lot of attention, I'm sure he'll stay put."

"I hope so," said Mom anxiously. "We don't want him to wander too far. If he starts going out in the road and along the sidewalks, he could easily get lost."

She glanced up at the clock. "I'd better get going. Have a wonderful day, all of you. Suzanne, do you want to invite that nice girl from your class to come over after school one day? What was her name? Izzie? I can call her mom. Maybe she could come tomorrow."

Dad nodded. "I can pick you all up from school."

Suzanne smiled. Dad had been so happy when she'd come home the day before and said she'd actually had a good day at school. She would really like Izzie to come over.

"I'll ask her," she agreed, tickling Boots behind the ears. He was sitting on her lap, hoping for bits of toast. He particularly liked toast with jelly, so Suzanne made sure she always had

72

jelly on at least one piece now. She tore off a little corner, and passed it down to him, watching him crunch it up and lick at his whiskers for crumbs.

"Do you really think Boots will be all right?" she asked Dad anxiously. "I don't want him to be lonely."

A cautious paw reached up onto the table, looking for more toast, and Dad snorted. "He'll be fine. He knows how to take care of himself very well. Don't you?" he added, scratching Boots under his little white chin. "Yes, you're so cute. Even if you are trying to steal yourself a second breakfast."

Boots drooped his whiskers, and stared at Dad, his blue eyes round and solemn.

Suzanne giggled. Boots made it look as though he were starving to death and even Dad was almost convinced. He glanced down at his own plate of toast, and then shook his head firmly.

"That kitten is a clever one!" he told Suzanne.

Boots prowled up and down the hallway, his tail twitching angrily. Suzanne had left him behind again, and now his cat flap was closed. He didn't understand what was happening. Why did she have to keep going away?

"Hey! Boots! Cat treats!" Suzanne's dad came out of the kitchen with a foil packet, and Boots turned around hopefully. He loved those treats, especially the fish-flavored ones. "Good boy. Yes, Suzanne said some of these might cheer you up."

Boots laid his ears back as he heard Suzanne's name, and stopped licking the treats out of Dad's hand. Suzanne! Was she about to come back? He looked at Dad hopefully.

"Oh, Boots. You really do miss her, don't you?" Dad eyed him worriedly. "She'll be back later, I promise. Come on, yummy fish treats."

Boots ate the rest of the treats slowly. He liked them, but he would have liked them much more if Suzanne had fed them to him. She had a game where she held them in front of his nose, one at a time, and he stretched up to reach. They didn't taste the same out of Dad's hand.

"Good boy, Boots." Dad picked him up gently, took him into the office, and put him down on an old armchair. "Why don't you take a nap?"

Boots walked around and around the seat of the chair, pushing his paws into the cushions, until eventually he slumped down and stared gloomily at the door. He didn't feel like sleeping, but he couldn't think of anything else to do.

Boots sat in front of the cat flap, staring at it hopefully, and uttering plaintive little meows. It was still locked. He knew because he'd tried it, over and over, scratching at the door with his claws. But it just wouldn't open.

"Do you need to go out?" Dad asked, coming into the kitchen, and looking at him, concerned. He crouched down next to Boots, who gave his knee a hopeful nudge. "I suppose it can't hurt. It's been more than an hour since Jackson and Suzanne left for school." Dad turned the latch on the cat flap and pushed it, showing Boots that it was open. "Go ahead."

Boots meowed gratefully, and wriggled through the cat flap, trotting purposefully out into the back yard, and straight around to the front of the house, just as he'd done the day before. Next, he was squeezing under the gate, and out into the road. This time he didn't run as fast. He knew that he'd been shut in the house for a long time, and he wouldn't be able to chase Suzanne the way he had yesterday.

So he padded down the path, sniffing thoughtfully here and there. It was difficult to follow the traces of Suzanne and Jackson—the house smelled like them, too, much more than the path, which made it confusing. But he was pretty sure that they'd gone this way. Boots bounded happily along, hoping that they would be in the field again, maybe sitting down, waiting for him.

But no one was there. Boots walked up and down the edge of the huge field, staring anxiously into the green stalks. Was Suzanne in there? She might be, but he couldn't smell her, or hear her. He slipped in between two rows of wheat, pushing his way through the green stalks, and meowing.

Then his ears twitched. There was a scuffling noise ahead of him, and a small bird fluttered out of the wheat, making Boots leap back in surprise. He'd seen birds in the yard, but never up close. He hissed at it angrily, but the bird was already half-hopping, half-flying away. Boots followed it sadly out of the wheat stalks. He didn't think Suzanne was here.

Glancing around the narrow path at the edge of the field, he tried to remember what Suzanne had been doing when he ran after her yesterday. They had been walking along here, away from him, as though they were heading for the hedge at the end of the field.

Determinedly, Boots padded along, hopping over the ruts and big clumps of grass, and keeping a hopeful eye out for Suzanne. At the corner of the field there was a gap in the hedge, and then a short muddy path, leading out on to a road with a sidewalk. Boots had never really seen a road, and he jumped back, his whiskers bristling, as a car roared past. He had been in a car when he left his mom to come to Suzanne's house, and then when he'd had to go to the vet for his vaccinations, but both times he had been in a cat carrier. From kitten height, the cars going along the road were enormous, and terrifyingly noisy.

He crept into the muddy path, eyeing the opening out on to the sidewalk. His ears were laid nervously back, but at the same time Boots breathed out the faintest little purr. The cars weren't the only noise he could hear. There was shouting, and laughter—the kind of noises Suzanne and Jackson made. He wasn't sure it was them, but it was worth looking. The sounds were coming from very close by. If he was brave enough to go out on to the sidewalk, close to those cars, he was sure he could find the place.

Boots dashed out, scurrying along low to the ground, and pressing as far into the hedge as he could go. Every time a car went past—which wasn't very often, thankfully—he buried himself under the prickly branches at the bottom of the hedge and peered out, his blue eyes round and fearful.

The school was only a couple of hundred feet along the main road through the town, and on the same side as the path. Boots squirmed under the metal fence at the side of the playground, and scuttled behind a wooden bench, where he sat, curled up as small as he could, and watched the children racing around the basketball court.

It was very noisy. He had thought Suzanne and Jackson were loud, but there were so many children here. And they were all wearing the same red cardigans and gray skirts, or shorts. He couldn't see Suzanne at all.

He shrank back behind the bench as a loud bell shrilled, and the children streamed back into the building on the far side of the playground. Then his ears pricked up, and he darted forward. That was Suzanne! Racing past him, with another girl. He meowed hopefully at her, but she'd already disappeared inside the white building.

The door was still open.

Boots padded out into the empty playground and hurried over to the door. The noise of the children still echoed around the hallway, and he shivered a little. But if he wanted to find Suzanne, this was where he needed to be. He padded along the chilly concrete floor, peeking in the doors when he found an open one. The first classroom he looked into was full of children who were smaller than Suzanne, he thought. A little boy stared at him, and pointed,

his eyes widening delightedly. Boots
scooted out the door as fast as he could.
He had a feeling that he wasn't meant
to be in here, and he didn't want to be
caught before he'd found Suzanne.

The next couple of doors were shut,
but then he found one ajar and looked
around it. These children were more
the right size. He sidled around the
door, and then he saw her, facing away
from him, but at the nearest table. The
children were all looking away from
the door, toward something at the
other end of the classroom, so it was
easy for Boots to race across the carpet
and hide under the table—right next
to Suzanne's feet. He purred quietly to
himself. He had done it! He'd found
her!

Very gently, he rubbed the side of his head against Suzanne's sock.

Suzanne gave a tiny squeak, and Izzie stared at her. "What's the matter?"

"Something under the table...," Suzanne whispered, her eyes horrified. It was furry. What if it was one of those enormous furry spiders? There were definitely more spiders in the country. She'd found a huge one in the bathroom over the weekend. Very slowly, she peered under the table, and Izzie looked, too.

"A cat!"

"Boots!"

Mrs. Mason looked around sharply, and Izzie and Suzanne tried to look at the board and pretend there wasn't anything under their table.

Boots purred louder, and patted at

Suzanne's leg with a velvety paw.

"What's he doing here?" Izzie whispered as soon as Mrs. Mason had turned back to the board.

"He must have followed us again." Suzanne was grinning. She couldn't help it. She wasn't quite sure how she was going to figure this out, but she loved it that Boots wanted to be with her so much that he followed her all the way to school.

Boots scrambled up on to her lap and sat there, purring, and nudging at her school cardigan.

Sarah and Missy saw a small orange head sticking up over the edge of the table and gasped. Suzanne put a finger to her lips and stared at them, pleading. "Don't tell!" she whispered.

Sarah and Missy shook their heads, to say of course they wouldn't. But Mrs. Mason had seen them anyway.

"Suzanne, what's going on?" She came over to their table. "Oh, my! A kitten! What's he doing here?"

"He followed me from home," said Suzanne. "I'm sorry, Mrs. Mason. He was under the table, and I didn't even know he was here until a minute ago."

She sighed, a very tiny sigh. She'd hoped to keep Boots a secret for a little longer.

Mrs. Mason smiled. "Well, he's very sweet, but I'm afraid he can't stay in the classroom. You'd better take him to the office and ask Mrs. Hart to call home. Is there someone who can come and get him?"

Suzanne nodded. "My dad." She stood up, with Boots snuggled against her, and the rest of the class whispered and aahed admiringly, reaching out to pet him as she went out of the classroom.

"You're so amazing for finding me!" Suzanne whispered, and Boots purred.

Chapter Six
Boots's Escape

"I can't believe you followed me all the way, Boots!" Suzanne told him again, as she cuddled him in between putting her shoes on for school the next day. "Everybody wanted to know about you. Even people in the grade above came to ask who you were—they saw me carrying you up to the office on their way back from PE." She sighed, and placed him down on the stairs so she could put on her other shoe. "But Miss Wilson made Dad promise he wouldn't let it happen again. He said Miss Wilson was really scary. You're going to hate being shut up for the whole day." She petted his head, looking at him worriedly. "I suppose in a few days you'll stop wanting to follow me. But I sort of wish you wouldn't. I love that you're so clever!"

Boots clambered up a couple of steps—it took a little while, as his legs were still pretty short—so that he could rub his chin on Suzanne's hair while she tied her shoe. He wasn't sure what she was saying, but it was definitely nice. She was fussing over him, and he liked to be fussed over.

Jackson came stomping down the hallway, and Suzanne turned around and dropped a kiss on the top of Boots's little furry head. "I've got to go. Be good, Boots!"

Boots sat on the steps and stared at her angrily as she slipped quickly out the front door, pulling it closed behind her. She had done it again! How many times did he have to follow them before she decided it would just be easier to take him with them? He jumped down the stairs in two huge leaps and ran for the cat flap. But it was locked. He scratched at it furiously until Dad came and picked him up.

"Sorry, Boots. Not happening, little one."

Boots wriggled out of his arms and stalked across the kitchen. He was going to follow Suzanne—somehow.

He would have to get out of the house a different way. Boots prowled thoughtfully through the different rooms, sniffing hopefully at the front door to see if it might open. He could smell outside, but the door was firmly shut. And so were all the windows.

But when Suzanne had taken him upstairs to play the day before, her window had been open. Boots sat at the

93

bottom of the stairs and gazed upward doubtfully. They were very big. But he could do it, if he was careful, and slow.

Determined, he began to scramble and haul himself up, stopping every once in a while to rest, until at last he heaved himself onto the landing. His legs felt wobbly, but he made himself keep going into Suzanne's room, where the door was open just a crack. As soon as he pushed his way around the door, his ears pricked forward excitedly. The window was open! Just as he had remembered it!

Forgetting how tired his legs were, Boots sprang up onto the bed, sniffing delightedly at the fresh air blowing in.

The windowsill was too far above the bed for him to reach, though. His whiskers drooped a little. How was he going to get up there? He padded up and down the bed and stared at Suzanne's pile of cuddly toys. She liked to tease him with them, walking them up and down the bed for him to pounce on. But why shouldn't he climb up them instead? He put out a cautious paw, testing the back of a fluffy toy cat. It squashed down a little, but it was still a step up, and then onto the back of a huge teddy bear, and the stuffed leopard … and the windowsill!

Boots pulled himself up, panting happily as he felt the cool breeze on his whiskers.

Now he just had to get down again on the outside....

"No kitten today?" Sarah asked Suzanne a little sadly.

Suzanne shook her head. "Miss Wilson made my dad promise he'd keep him in. Poor Boots. He's going to be so upset."

"He's the cleverest cat I've ever seen," Sarah told her admiringly. "Imagine coming all that way! And he'd never even been to the school before—I don't know how he figured out where to go!"

Suzanne smiled. "It's amazing, isn't it? I think he must have heard us all in the playground."

"You should stop by the store and buy him a treat on the way home," Izzie suggested. "I've got some money, if you don't have any on you."

Suzanne nodded. "It's okay, thanks. I've got some. That's a really good idea." She grinned at Izzie. "You can help me choose." It was so nice having a good friend to hang out with—it felt like being back at her old school. Izzie's mom had been fine with Izzie walking with Suzanne—Izzie usually walked home, too. She had an older sister in Jackson's class.

"He might even start talking to us if we bring him cat treats...."

Boots scrambled frantically at the branches of the bush. It had looked so solid and easy to climb. But it turned out to be much harder to get down than up. It was also more wobbly, and he didn't like that. The first part had been easy, just a little jump to that sloping part of the roof, then across the tiles. It was the drop down from the roof that was the problem. His claws were slipping. Boots gave up trying to hang on and leaped out, as far away from the wall as he could, hoping that he remembered how to land.

He hit the ground with a jolt, but he was there! In the front yard, right by the gate and the road. Boots darted a glance behind him. Then he scrambled under the gate and set off to find Suzanne, trotting along jauntily. He knew the way now; he didn't have to sniff and search and worry.

He was halfway down the field when it started to rain. A very large drop hit him on the nose, making him shrink back. It was soon followed by a lot of others, and in seconds his fur was plastered flat over his thin ribs. He hid in the hedge, his ears laid back.

He would wait for it to stop, Boots decided, gazing out disgustedly. He certainly didn't want to go anywhere in that. But it went on and on, and he needed to find Suzanne. He put his nose out cautiously, and shivered as he felt the drops on his whiskers. It was horrible.

But he couldn't stay here all day….

At last he slunk out from under the bush, plodding through the wet, muddy ruts, and hoping that Suzanne would have something warm and dry to wrap around him when he got to the school. He scurried down the pavement, through the puddles, so miserable that he didn't even bother to dart under the bush to avoid the car going past. The driver of the car didn't see the soaked little kitten, and even if he had, he probably wouldn't have been able to avoid the huge puddle that splashed up over Boots like a wave. There was so much water that he staggered back, letting out a cold, sad meow. Then he flat out ran for the school, racing across the playground toward that warm, open door.

But it was closed.

It had been wet at recess, and no one had wanted the rain blowing in. All the doors were closed—every single one, as the soaked, orange-striped kitten found when he ran frantically all the way around the building.

Remembering the window he had climbed out of at home, Boots looked up to see if there were any he could get through. There was a bench up against the wall, with a window right above it, and he jumped for the seat, scrambling desperately until he could heave himself up. Then it was a little hop onto the arm of the bench,

101

and then again onto the windowsill. But the window was shut, and everyone was gathered together at the other end of the classroom, looking at something and talking excitedly. They didn't hear him scratching hopefully at the window, and at last he jumped down.

Boots sat under the bench and meowed miserably, calling for someone to come and let him in. He didn't care if they took him back home again, as long as he was out of the rain. He would stay at home, and never try to follow anyone, if only he were dry.

No one came. No one heard him over the hammering and splashing of the rain, and the water from the bench was dripping all over him. Boots crawled out, looking around for another place to hide. There were trees over on the edge of the path to the field. Maybe it would be drier there. He ran through the wet grass, shivering as the stems rubbed along his soaked fur, and shaking water drops off his whiskers. He was so cold. Sitting still under the bench had made him shiver, and now he couldn't stop.

Then something made his ears flick up a little. There was another building. Just a little one, a shed, and he could see that the door was open!

Boots made one last effort, forcing his shaky paws to race to the shed, and struggle over the step and into the dusty dryness. He was so relieved to be out of the rain that he hardly noticed the sports equipment piled up all over the place— just the heap of old, tattered mats that he could curl up on to take a nap.

It was while Boots was fast asleep that the custodian remembered that he hadn't locked up the shed when he'd taken out the extra chairs, and came grumpily back through the rain with his keys.

Chapter Seven
Lost and Alone

"Boots!" Suzanne called happily, as she opened the front door to let herself and Izzie and Jackson inside. "Boots, come and meet Izzie!"

Dad hurried out of the kitchen, a worried expression on his face. "You didn't see him in the road?"

Suzanne stared at him, not understanding. "What?" she asked, with a frown.

"Boots! He's not out there? I wondered if he'd slipped out somehow. He must have, because I can't find him anywhere." Dad glanced distractedly up and down the hallway, as though he thought Boots might pop out from behind the boots.

"You—you can't find him?" Suzanne stammered. "You mean—he's lost?"

"I'm sorry, Suzanne." Dad ran his fingers through his hair until it stood up on end. "I had a long phone meeting all morning that finished about an hour ago. Then I went to find Boots and check that he was all right, but he'd disappeared. I just don't understand how he could have gotten out!"

"Maybe he didn't," Izzie suggested

shyly. "He could be shut in somewhere. Oscar's always doing that. He climbed into a drawer once and went to sleep, and my mom didn't see him and she shut the drawer. Then she got a real shock because her dresser was meowing."

"Maybe...," Dad murmured. But he looked doubtful. "Let's check again."

Suzanne grabbed Izzie's hand and pulled her up the stairs, while Jackson hurried into the living room.

"Bathroom," Suzanne muttered. "Not in here. The linen closet, maybe?" She pulled the door open, but no kitten darted out. "Jackson's room...." She peered in and called, "Boots! Boots! He isn't here, Izzie. I'm sure he'd come if he heard me calling. Or he'd meow to tell me where he was."

"He could be asleep. Try the other rooms, just in case."

Suzanne peered into her mom and dad's room, opening the dresser and all the drawers, but there weren't even any orange hairs. "This is my room," she told Izzie, pushing the last door open. "Boots!" Suzanne caught her breath. She'd been hoping to find him asleep on her bed, but he wasn't there.

"Your window's open…," Izzie said slowly.

"Oh, but he couldn't get out through that." Suzanne shook her head. "It's really high."

Izzie frowned. "It depends how much he wanted to."

The girls climbed onto the bed so that they could look out the window.

"You see? He could jump on there."
Izzie pointed toward the low part of
the roof. "And there's all that ivy stuff.
That's like a cat ladder."

Suzanne stared at her. "You think he
really could have climbed down that?"

Izzie looked down at the grass, which
was a very long way down. "He might
have."

Dad came in, with Jackson behind.
"He isn't in the house," Dad said grimly.
"Was that window open, Suzanne?"

"Yes!" Suzanne nodded, her eyes filling
with tears. "I'm really sorry, Dad!
I didn't think Boots would try
to climb out of it! He can hardly
get up the stairs, and
the windowsill's
really high."

"It isn't your fault." Dad put an arm around her. "I should have checked on him earlier. None of us realized he would be able to climb out of the window." He leaned over to look out. "I think he did, though. Some of that bush has been torn away."

"Can we go and look for him?" Suzanne asked. "He might have tried to get to school again, and gotten lost…. Oh, Dad, what if he went out on the road?"

Dad hugged her tighter. "Don't panic, Suzanne. I don't think he would, because he's scared of the car noises. Remember how he meowed when we got him out of the car at the vet? Even though he was safe in his basket, he didn't like it when the cars went past. And why would he get confused about the way to school, when he made it yesterday?" He let go of Suzanne and headed for the door. "I'm just going to call the school and see if he's turned up there."

Suzanne sank down on her bed, staring up at Izzie. "I can't believe it. Everyone's been telling me today how lucky I am, and how beautiful Boots is, and now he's gone. I've only had him a couple of weeks, Izzie! How could I have lost him?"

It was starting to get dark. Boots scratched at the door with his claws again, but they were starting to hurt. He'd hoped that he could make that little thin strip of light and fresh air bigger, maybe even big enough to squeeze through. But all he'd managed to do was scratch off some of the paint. Miserably, he sank down, meowing faintly. No one seemed to hear him, and it had been a long time since he'd last heard anyone outside.

Maybe he would have to stay here all night, he thought anxiously. Suzanne wouldn't know where he was. Maybe she was looking for him. He stood up again quickly, even though his paws felt sore, and meowed as loudly as he could. Suzanne would look for him, he was sure of it.

But even though he called and called and called to her, she didn't come, and at last he had to give up. He was worn out

112

from scratching and meowing, and he dragged his sore paws back to the pile of mats. Then he curled up into a tight little ball and lay there in the gathering darkness, wondering how long it would be before anyone found him.

"We can make some 'lost' posters," Izzie suggested the next morning. "If we ask Mrs. Mason, I bet she'll let us use the computer to make the fliers. We could put them up all around town on the way home."

Suzanne nodded. She should have thought of that the night before. After Izzie had gone home, she and Jackson had searched the house all over again, and then Suzanne had gone to bed and cried herself to sleep, knowing that her little kitten wasn't curled up in his basket in the kitchen—he was out there in the dark, and she had no idea where.

"We could go to the houses between here and school and ask if anyone's seen him," she suggested, shivering at the thought of poor Boots wandering around lost somewhere.

"Good idea," Izzie agreed. "We could get people to check their garages. Don't worry, Suzanne. I can help with that. I know almost everybody in town, and it's scary if you don't know people."

"That would be great," Suzanne said. She'd do anything if it meant finding Boots, even if she had to talk to hundreds of people she didn't know.

A couple of the middle-school girls came past Suzanne and Izzie on their way in. "Hey, Suzanne! Did you get into trouble with Miss Wilson yesterday?" one of them asked.

Suzanne stared at her in bewilderment. "W-what?" she muttered, suddenly shy.

"When your kitten came back! I thought your brother said that Miss Wilson was angry, and she told your dad that he had to keep your kitten at home."

Suzanne forgot all about being shy. "You mean you saw Boots? Are you sure it was yesterday?" she asked the older girl eagerly.

"Yeah, definitely...." The older girl— Suzanne was pretty sure her name was Emma—frowned. "I saw him looking in the classroom window, but then he ran off. Why? What's the matter?"

"Boots is lost," Suzanne explained. "Dad had him in the house, but he climbed out of a window. We think he must have tried to follow us. We weren't sure he had made it to school, but if you saw him, then he was definitely here!"

"You're not mixing up the days?" Izzie asked Emma doubtfully.

Emma shook her head. "Nope. I'm certain. It was yesterday when it was raining. And your kitten was soaked. His fur was actually dripping. I saw him out the window; he was in the playground. Before recess, I think."

"He must have gotten out the window really soon after we left," Suzanne said. "Thank you, Emma! I have to go and look for him!"

Chapter Eight
The Big Search

There was sunlight coming in from somewhere else, Boots noticed, as the shed grew slowly lighter that morning. It wasn't just the space around the door. Where there was light, maybe there was some sort of hole, or another window that might be open, so he could climb through it.

It was up at the top, near the ceiling,

he saw. Very high up. Much higher than Suzanne's window. But then, there were a lot more things to climb in here. Piles of chairs, some benches, and more of those mats. He'd just have to find a way to reach it.

Boots was sure that Suzanne was looking for him—almost sure, anyway. But the shed was all the way across the field from the school, he'd realized, as he lay curled up on the mats. What if Suzanne didn't know about it? He couldn't wait for someone to let him out. He would have to do it himself.

He stretched out his paws, which felt a little better this morning, though they still ached from all that scratching. Then he padded across the pile of mats, and made a wobbly jump onto an old wooden bench. That was the first step....

"Where do we start?" Izzie asked, as they hurried across the playground.

"I don't know. Maybe we should find Jackson and tell him that those girls saw Boots," Suzanne suggested, but she couldn't see her brother anywhere, and she wanted to start searching. "My dad called yesterday, remember? And he spoke to Mrs. Hart in the office, and she asked in the staff room. No one had seen Boots. So he wasn't just hanging around school looking for us."

Izzie frowned. "I know I keep going

on about him being shut in somewhere, but...."

Suzanne shook her head. "No, I think you're right! It's the only thing that makes sense. But where?"

Izzie shook her head. "I don't know. Maybe the classroom closets? Do you think if we asked Mrs. Hart we could go and look? Oh, no! There's the bell."

Suzanne looked anxiously around as everyone began to collect his or her stuff and head into school. "I can't go into school now! I can't! Boots is here somewhere. I know he is!"

Izzie patted her shoulder. "It's okay. Look, we'll tell Mrs. Mason that Boots might be here. We have to go in, Suzanne. Otherwise, we'll get in trouble."

Suzanne almost didn't care, but she supposed Izzie was right. Maybe they could ask the principal what to do. She'd said her dog used to follow her to school. She'd understand.

But Miss Wilson was talking to one of the other teachers, and she just waved the girls past when Suzanne tried to hover in the doorway and talk to her.

Mrs. Mason was late coming into their class, and when she finally arrived she had her arms full of colored shirts for PE, and she didn't look like she wanted to hear about kittens, even though Izzie tried her best.

"Oh, dear…. Well, I'm sure you can take a look at recess," she said distractedly when the girls tried to explain. "Sit down, please, you two."

Sit down! Suzanne opened her mouth to argue, but Mrs. Mason wasn't even looking at her anymore.

"Once I've taken attendance, everyone, I've got some exciting news— we're going to start practicing for Sports Day. We've scheduled a couple of extra PE sessions, and the first one is this morning. So let's just mark everyone here…." She moved names around on the whiteboard. "Where's Keisha? Is she still sick? Okay."

"I don't want to do PE," Suzanne whispered frantically. "I have to go and look for Boots!"

"PE!" Izzie nudged her. "I just thought of something! Shut up in a shed, Suzanne—we said he might be!"

"What are you talking about?" Suzanne was fighting back tears.

"There's a little shed at the end of the field where Mr. Larkin, the custodian, keeps stuff that doesn't get used very often. He was definitely carrying chairs in and out yesterday; I heard him complaining about how wet he'd gotten."

"So the shed was open?" Suzanne breathed, her eyes widening.

Izzie nodded. "It must have been."

"Now go and get changed, please, everyone," Mrs. Mason called. "Then we'll go to the gym, as it's still a little too wet on the field."

"I'm not getting changed," Suzanne

said, glaring at Izzie as though she thought her friend might argue. "I'm going to find Boots."

Izzie shrugged. "Uh-huh, and I'm coming with you. Come on."

They hurried out of the classroom, ahead of everyone else, and Izzie grabbed Suzanne's hand. "It's this way. There's a side door; come on." She pulled Suzanne down the hallway and pushed open a door that Suzanne hadn't even known about. "This is a quick way out to the field."

"Hey, Izzie!" someone called. "We're in the gym, not the field! And you aren't changed!"

But Izzie and Suzanne were already running across the damp grass.

Boots wobbled on the old chair. He was almost there—he could see the narrow wooden windowsill and the dirty pane of glass. The wind was shaking it, as though it were loose. If he could only get to it, maybe he could push his way out, somehow....

He balanced himself again, teetering on the edge of the chair. He'd scrambled his way up the whole pile, and it had taken so long. If he misjudged his jump to the window, he wasn't sure he'd have the strength to climb up again. He was so hungry, and tired, and his paws hurt.

His whiskers flicked and shook as he tried to figure out how he could make the jump. It was much further than he'd ever jumped before. And the strip of

125

wood along the window was very small. But if it meant that he could get out…. Then he would go back home, and wait there for Suzanne. He would see if he could get back in through the cat flap.

He tensed his muscles to spring, and crouched there, trembling a little, trying to summon the courage to leap.

Then his ears twitched. He could hear someone! People, talking!

"Boots! Boots, are you in there? Is the door locked, Izzie?"

That was Suzanne!

Boots let out a shrill, desperate meow, and forgot to worry about how narrow the ledge was. He just went for it, scrambling madly with his paws as he almost made it, and then heaving himself up onto the windowsill.

Then he batted his paws against the glass, meowing frantically.

"I can hear him! He's in there, Izzie! You were right!"

"It's locked. I'll go and get Mr. Larkin."

Boots heard feet thudding away and cried out in panic. They hadn't heard him! They were leaving!

"It's okay, Boots. Where are you?"

There were noises outside and Boots banged his nose against the grubby window, trying to see what was happening.

Suzanne pulled herself up onto the tiny ledge on the outside of the window. "I can see you! It's really you, Boots! Oh, I've been so worried. I can't believe you climbed out of a window." She giggled with relief, and sniffed. "And now you're trying to climb out of this one, aren't you, silly kitten."

Boots meowed and scraped, but the window wouldn't open. How was he going to get to Suzanne?

"Oh! Mr. Larkin! The keys!" Suzanne's face disappeared from the window, and Boots wriggled himself around as the door rattled and shook. And then it opened.

With a joyful yowl, he bounded back to the wobbly chair, and took a flying leap to the mats, and then Suzanne was there, hugging him.

Boots purred and purred, and rubbed his face against hers, and purred louder.

"Izzie! Suzanne! What are you doing out here? Oh! Oh, no, has he been shut in here?" Mrs. Mason peered worriedly into the dusty shed.

"All night," Suzanne told her, shivering. "Can I call my dad, Mrs. Mason, please? Can I take him home?"

Mrs. Mason nodded. "Yes, you'd better take him up to the office again. I hope he doesn't keep doing this, Suzanne."

Suzanne petted Boots, who was pressed against her sweater like he never meant to let go. "Me, too."

"Well, he got soaking wet and trapped in a shed, so maybe he'll stay home now," Izzie suggested.

Suzanne nodded. "He looks like he wants to go home," she agreed, feeling the sharp little points of Boots's claws hooked into her sweater. "I promise I won't ever let you get lost again," she whispered to him, feeling his whiskers brush across her cheek. "I'll take care of you forever."

"I'm really glad my mom said I could come back with you." Izzie sighed happily and blew on her hot chocolate.

Suzanne nodded, petting Boots, who was curled up on her lap, with his claws hooked determinedly into her school skirt. He wasn't letting her go. "We might never have figured out where he was if it hadn't been for you! He could have been stuck in there for a really long time—until Mr. Larkin had to put the chairs away again."

Boots purred as Suzanne gently rubbed behind his ears. He was finally starting to feel warm again. Suzanne's dad had lit the fire in the living room, and the girls were huddled in front of it—it was raining again, so it had been a wet walk home. They'd splashed through the puddles as fast as they could, anxious to see Boots again, and check that he was okay.

"Do you want any more hot chocolate, girls?" Dad asked. "Jackson's getting another cup."

Suzanne shook her head. "No, thanks."

Izzie smiled at him. "No, that's okay, thanks. It was delicious. It's too bad that cats can't have hot drinks, though. Boots must have been frozen after spending the night in the shed."

"I've had him on my lap ever since I picked him up," Dad told them. "Except for when he was wolfing down a huge dinner and breakfast in one. He definitely wanted company, and since he couldn't have you, Suzanne, I was the next best thing."

"I hope he's not going to follow us again tomorrow," Suzanne said, looking down at him anxiously. He didn't look very adventurous at the moment....

Dad shook his head. "No, I'm sure he'll remember being trapped. He won't want that to happen again. But I promise I will make sure every window's closed. I'll even let him play with the computer, Suzanne." He grinned. "I'll find him one of those homework websites. Then he won't need to go to school."

Boots stretched out his paws and stared up at everyone in surprise as they laughed, and then once again he curled himself into the front of Suzanne's sweater. It was cozy and warm inside. And dry. He hadn't realized how damp and miserable it could be, following people. For the moment, he was going to stay right here.

The
Unwanted
Kitten

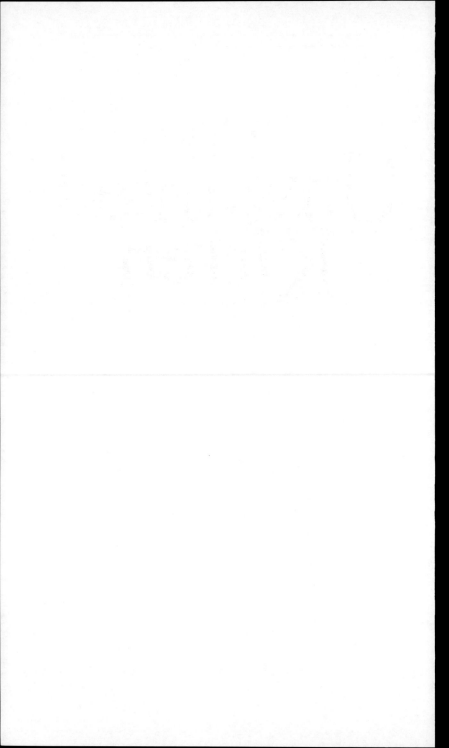

Contents

For Lucy

Chapter One
The Big Move

As the car started, Lucy pressed her face up against the window, staring sadly back at her home. Except it wasn't her home anymore. In a few hours' time another family would arrive, and another moving truck, just like the one that was lumbering down the road in front of her parents' car. She blinked back tears as they pulled away, staring back at Nutmeg and Ginger, the two friendly cats from the house next door. They'd been frightened away by all the noise, but now they were back in their usual spot, the wall between Lucy's yard and the one next door. They liked to sunbathe on the bricks, and Lucy loved to play with them and cuddle them and pretend they were hers. She longed to have a cat of her own. She had asked her parents so many times, but they always said she would have to wait until she was older.

The orange cats stared curiously after the car. Lucy rolled down her window and waved to them. Nutmeg meowed and walked down the wall toward the street. Lucy sniffed miserably.

She couldn't believe she would never
see them again. A few seconds later the
car turned out of her road and
she could no longer see
the cats, or even
the house.

"How long until we get there?" Ethan, Lucy's older brother, asked, unplugging his new iPod for a moment.

"A couple of hours, probably," their mom said. "We should definitely be settling in by lunchtime!"

"Doesn't it feel great, being on our way to our new home!" their dad added enthusiastically.

Lucy sniffed and said nothing. She clutched Stripy, her old toy cat, even tighter. They'd just left her home behind. What they were going to was only a horrible *house*. It would never, ever be home.

Lucy hardly spoke the entire time. She just gazed out of the window, and worried. A new house. A new school. No friends! She missed Ellie, her best friend, so much already. Ellie would be in the middle of PE right now. *I wonder if she's missing me, too,* Lucy thought.

"We're almost there!" her mom said excitedly, jerking Lucy out of her daydream, where she was back at school playing soccer with Ellie. "Look, Lucy! This is our street! Doesn't it look beautiful?"

Lucy made a small *mmm* sort of noise. It was nice. Pretty yards and friendly-looking houses. But it wasn't home.

"Oh, good, the movers are here already! Let's start getting unpacked. I bet you two want to see your rooms, don't you?" Dad sounded even more enthusiastic than Mom, if that were possible.

Lucy's new room was huge — much bigger than her old one, as Mom had happily pointed out. "And you can have it any color you want, Lucy," she promised, placing a box of toys on the floor. "Maybe purple. What do you think?"

Lucy sat on the bed that the movers had dumped in the corner and gazed around, hugging Stripy. She was trying to be happy, but it was all so different.

The weekend flew past in a messy, grubby whirl of unpacking. Lucy felt left out — Mom and Dad were so happy about the move, and even Ethan was excited about the new house. She seemed to be the only one who missed home.

Now the moment she was really dreading had arrived — her first day at her new school. Surely someone who'd just moved should get at least a week off from school, not just one Friday, spent driving to the new house. Even Ethan had complained that it wasn't fair they had to start their new schools today. Lucy trailed slowly across the empty playground after her mom, who was heading for the school office.

"Look, a school garden!" Mom said brightly. "And the sign says they have a gardening club. You'd love that, helping to plant seeds, wouldn't you?"

"Maybe," Lucy muttered. She saw a notice up about a soccer team, too, but there was no way she'd be able to join a team now, in the middle of the school year. *Everyone will already have their friends, and their groups,* she thought unhappily. *I'm going to be so left out.*

The school secretary buzzed them in and took them over to Lucy's classroom. The school was actually much newer than the one Lucy had been going to until three days before, but she wished she were back at her old school. She stayed silent as her mom and the secretary chatted about the new computer suite. Her mouth was drooping sadly as they arrived at class 5W, and the secretary showed them in.

Her new teacher, Mrs. Walker, smiled kindly at her, then announced, "Class, I'd like you to meet Lucy. She just moved here, and I want you all to make her feel very welcome."

Lucy blushed and didn't know where to look. She hated having everyone staring at her. Mrs. Walker then took Lucy aside and said the class had really been looking forward to having her and she knew Lucy would be very happy once she'd settled in.

Lucy wasn't sure how she was supposed to do that — she'd never had to settle in anywhere before. She'd been to the same school since kindergarten, and she had known *everyone*.

"You sit here, Lucy, and Olivia and Katie will help you," Mrs. Walker said. "You'll show Lucy where everything is, won't you, girls?"

Olivia and Katie nodded and smiled. "Hi, Lucy!" they chorused.

"Hello," Lucy muttered, and sat

down as quickly as she could.

Olivia and Katie tried their best, but Lucy was too shy to give more than yes or no answers to their polite questions. Eventually they gave up, and although they stayed with her through lunchtime, they stopped bothering to talk to her. *They don't like me*, Lucy told herself unhappily, as she listened silently to Olivia telling Katie all about her ballet exam. *No one's even talking to me.*

Class 5W were actually quite a friendly group, but they couldn't do much faced with a silent Lucy, and she was so unhappy that she couldn't see that she needed to make an effort, too. Lucy was in the coatroom putting on her coat to go home, when she heard some of the girls talking about her. She stayed frozen where she was, hidden behind a coat rack, and listened.

"That new girl is a little strange," someone said, giggling.

"Yeah, she hardly said a word all day." Lucy recognized the voice of Olivia, one of the girls who was showing her around. "I hope Mrs. Walker doesn't make us stay with her tomorrow, too."

"Maybe she thinks she's too good for us," another voice suggested. "I'm glad I didn't have to talk to her."

"Yeah, she does seem a bit stuck-up," Olivia agreed.

Another girl from Lucy's class who was on the same side of the coatroom as her gave Lucy a worried look, and coughed loudly. There was a sudden silence, then

Olivia's head popped around the coats, and her eyes went saucer-wide. She shot back again, and there was a burst of embarrassed giggling.

Lucy stood up and stalked out, blinking back tears. So what if they didn't like her? She certainly didn't like *them*. She heard the girls start whispering very fast, worrying about her telling Mrs. Walker what they'd said. *I hate this school*, she thought, as she brushed her sleeve across her face angrily, trying to pretend to herself and everybody else that she wasn't crying.

"So how was your first day? Did you have a good time?" her mom asked eagerly as she met Lucy at the school gate.

153

"No. It was horrible, and I want to go home."

"Oh, Lucy, I'm sorry." Her mom looked at her anxiously. "I'm sure it'll get better, honestly. You just need to take a few days to get used to everything." She sighed, and then said in a cheerful voice, "I thought we'd walk back. It's not far. Ethan wanted to go by himself, so you and I can see if we find any nice parks on the way home."

"Not there, *home*. I want to go back to our old house, and my old school. I hate it here! No one likes me!" Lucy wailed. "I miss Ellie, and all my friends!"

Mom sighed again. "Lucy, your dad and I have explained this. We had to move. Dad's job is here now, and if we lived in our old house, he'd have to spend hours getting to work. We'd never see him. You wouldn't like that, would you?"

Lucy shook her head and sniffed, trying not to cry where lots of people from school would see her. "I know," she whispered. "But it's really awful here."

Her mom put an arm around her shoulder. "I know it's hard, sweetheart. But I promise it *will* get better. We'll just have to do lots of fun things to cheer you up."

Lucy rubbed her sleeve across her eyes. She couldn't believe she had to go back tomorrow.

Chapter Two
A Special Present

Lucy stared out of the classroom window, trying not to catch anyone's eye. She'd been at her new school for almost a week now, but she still hadn't settled in. She couldn't forget the way Olivia had talked about her. The awful thing was, Lucy knew she probably had seemed stuck-up and unfriendly, and all those things Olivia had said. But it still seemed unfair. Didn't they know how lonely she was? Couldn't they see how difficult it was being the new girl? *At least it's Friday*, Lucy thought.

"Hey! Pssst...."

Lucy jumped slightly as someone poked her hand. She looked up, confused. The pretty red-haired girl who sat across the table from her in her math group had poked her with a pencil.

"Mrs. Walker's watching you," the red-haired girl whispered. "If you weren't new, she'd have said something to you by now. You've been looking out the window for a long time, and we're supposed to be drawing that hexagon shape. Are you stuck? Do you need an eraser or something?"

Lucy shook her head, and gave her a tiny smile. "I'm okay, thanks," she whispered back, glancing quickly over at Mrs. Walker. It was true — the teacher was looking her way. She bent her head over her book, suddenly feeling a little less miserable. Maybe there were some nice people in her new class after all.

When the bell rang for recess, Lucy watched as the red-haired girl wandered out of the classroom with a group of other girls, all chatting excitedly. Maybe she should say something to her. But that would mean going up to her in front of the entire group. She would have to try to say something interesting, or just hang around on the edge of the circle until someone noticed her. She couldn't face that; what if they all ignored her? Lucy gave a little shudder and stayed put. She'd go to the school library. Like she had every other day this week.

The next morning, Lucy lay in bed, hugging Stripy, and feeling grateful that she didn't have to drag herself out to get ready for school. She'd tried to go back to sleep, but it wasn't working. She sighed, and looked around her room. So far she hadn't even bothered to unpack all her boxes. She was still hoping that somehow things would change and they could go home, but the hope was draining away with every day they stayed.

Ethan wasn't helping, either. He loved his new school, and last night he'd spent most of dinner time talking enthusiastically about going to play football with some really cool new friends he'd made already. Mom was really excited about all the decorating that needed to be done, and Dad had started his new job…. Only Lucy was desperate to go back to their old home.

"Lucy! Hey!" It was Ethan, banging on her door.

Lucy ignored him, but he didn't go away. "Lucy! Get up, lazy!" He opened her door a crack, and peered in.

Lucy sat up. "Out! You're not allowed in my room!"

"Okay, okay! But get up. Mom and Dad have a surprise for you in the kitchen. You're going to love it!" he called, then thumped off back downstairs again.

A surprise! For a tiny moment Lucy's heart leaped. They were going home after all! She jumped out of bed and raced down after Ethan.

"Are we going home?" she gasped excitedly, catching him just at the bottom of the stairs.

Ethan gave her a strange look. "Of course not, silly. This *is* home now."

Lucy's shoulders slumped again. She trailed into the kitchen after him.

"Lucy!" Her parents were smiling happily at her, which just made Lucy feel more alone than ever.

"We've got a surprise for you, darling. Remember we said you'd have a special treat when we got here?" Mom pointed to a large box on the kitchen table.

Lucy stared dully at it. When her parents told them about the move, they'd said they would get Ethan an iPod, and that they had a special present in mind for Lucy, too. She'd been so sad missing everyone at home that she'd forgotten all about it.

She stared at the box, feeling just the tiniest bit excited. What could be inside? Suddenly the box started squeaking.

Lucy moved closer, curious despite herself. She opened the top flaps, which were attached together to make a sort of handle, and peered in.

Inside the box was the most beautiful creature Lucy had ever seen. A kitten with soft creamy fur, huge blue eyes, a chocolate-brown nose and oversized brown ears.

Lucy gasped. A kitten!

The kitten looked anxiously up as the box opened, and meowed. It was a strange noise, almost like a baby crying, and Lucy immediately wanted to pick up the kitten and cuddle it. The kitten seemed to think this was a good idea, too. It stood up, balancing its paws on the side of the box, and shyly put its head over the side, looking up at Lucy with its amazing sapphire-blue eyes. "Wowl?" it asked pleadingly. "Wowl!"

Lucy lifted out the kitten, and it immediately snuggled into her pajama top and started to purr. "Hello, little one," she said softly.

"Told you she'd love her," Lucy's dad said happily to her mom. "Her name is Sky, Lucy. She's a Siamese. We know you've wanted a kitten for so long, and we think you're old enough now to take care of a cat properly."

"Yes," said Mom. "We know how upset you've been about us moving to Fairfield. But you can't be miserable with a beautiful kitten to play with, can you?"

Lucy stared at them in disbelief. The kitten was beautiful, but it was as if her parents thought having a pet would suddenly make everything all right again. Lucy would forget about Ellie and all her friends, her school, her old bedroom, and be happy forever. Her eyes filled with angry, disappointed tears.

She carefully detached the kitten's tiny, needle-sharp claws from her pajamas, and put her back in the box. Then she ran out of the kitchen, her shoulders heaving.

166

"Lucy!" Mom called after her, her voice shocked.

"Hey, Lucy, what's the matter?" Ethan said. "Mom, Dad, can I pick the kitten up? It's really cute, and it's crying."

Dad's voice was worried as he answered. "Yes, go ahead, Ethan. I need to talk to Lucy and find out what's wrong. I just don't understand. I was sure she'd be so happy."

Chapter Three
A Confusing Welcome

Lucy's dad had picked up Sky from the breeder early that morning. Sky had only left home before to go to the vet, and she'd always returned to her familiar room, and the big basket she shared with her mom and her brothers and sisters. Today she'd had to stay in the dark box on her own for a long time, and she was so lonely. She wished she could go home, and snuggle up and let her mom lick her fur to make her feel better.

Where was she? It didn't smell like the vet, and it certainly wasn't home. She couldn't hear any other cats, either. She had started to cry for her home and her mom, and then someone had opened the box.

Sky shrank back into the corner of the box and peered up at the girl, feeling scared. Who was this? It wasn't one of the people she had met before. But then the girl, Lucy, had picked her up, and Sky had relaxed a little. She could see the delight in the girl's eyes, hear it in her quickened breathing, and feel it in the thud of her heart as the girl held her close. She had nestled snugly up against her, purring gratefully. She liked this person. The girl had petted her, and rubbed her lovingly under her chin. But then suddenly she had taken her firmly around the middle, and put her back into that dark box.

Sky didn't understand. She had *felt* how happy the girl was to hold her. Lucy had been full of love; she knew it. Why had she suddenly changed her mind?

Now she was sitting in a large, comfortable basket in the corner of the kitchen, with a bowl of kitten food and another bowl of water. There was a litter box close by. She had everything she needed. But no one was with her, and she was so lonely. What had she done wrong? When Lucy had run out, the boy had cuddled her briefly, then everyone had disappeared, and the kitchen was empty.

Sky was not used to being on her own. Until early this morning, she had lived in a house that was full of cats — her mom, and all her mom's sisters

171

and their kittens, and her own sisters and brothers. Sky had spent most of her time with her mom, snuggling up in their basket, but she enjoyed being petted by people as well.

She wouldn't have minded leaving her home so much if Lucy had kept cuddling her, but now that she was alone, she felt desperate to go back. She howled her loud, piercing, Siamese howl, crying for someone to come and love her.

Upstairs in her room, Lucy could hear Sky. The kitten's sad, lonely wails made her want to cry, too. She knew exactly how Sky felt — taken away from her cozy home, and brought somewhere she didn't belong. She wished she could go and comfort her, but she just couldn't do it.

Lucy could hear her parents coming up the stairs, talking in low, worried voices, and she knew she had to explain how she was feeling. The trouble was, she wasn't sure she *could*. Maybe it would be easier just to say she'd changed her mind about wanting a cat?

Her parents came in and sat next to her on her bed. Her mom put an arm around her, but Lucy sat stiff and tense.

"I'm sorry, but I don't want a kitten," she said tiredly when Dad asked what was wrong.

Her parents exchanged confused glances. "But Lucy, you've begged for one for years!" Mom protested. "Every Christmas and birthday, a kitten has been at the top of your list. Now we've finally moved to a house big enough to have a cat, and on a nice quiet road, and you've changed your mind!"

"Yes, I've changed my mind," Lucy echoed.

"We thought you'd love a kitten," Dad said, shaking his head. "All that time you used to spend playing with Nutmeg and Ginger next door. Mrs. Jones used to joke that they were more your cats than hers."

Lucy's eyes filled with tears again at the thought of Nutmeg and Ginger. She missed them so much.

There was another mournful cry from downstairs. "That poor kitten," Mom said. "She doesn't know what's going on. We'd better go down so she isn't all alone. Lucy, I know you're missing our old home, but we thought Sky would cheer you up. She really needs someone to take care of her."

Lucy didn't answer. She knew that! She was desperate to go and cuddle Sky, and tell her everything would be all right. But things weren't all right, and it was no use pretending.

Lucy glanced up as her parents shut the door. As soon as she was sure that they were both at least halfway down the stairs, she buried her head in her pillow and cried and cried. A kitten! At last! And she couldn't keep her!

Eventually, Lucy dragged herself up from her bed. She wanted someone to talk to — she wanted Ellie! Lucy took out a pen and her favorite cat writing paper from one of the boxes, and started to write to her about everything.

Hi Ellie!

Mom and Dad have just given me a beautiful Siamese kitten - she's so cute and soft to cuddle, and she's got the biggest blue eyes you've ever seen. I should be really happy, but the thing is I can't keep her! They think giving me a kitten will make me cheer up, and not miss home and you and all my friends. Mom even said so! Well, that's not going to happen.

Lucy started to cry again, and her tears smudged the ink on the page. She scrunched up the unfinished letter and threw it in the garbage can. It was just so unfair! A beautiful kitten, just like she had always wanted, but her parents had only gotten Sky to make Lucy forget her real home.

"Well, I won't!" Lucy muttered fiercely, gulping back sobs. "They can't make me! Not even with a kitten…."

By now Lucy had cried so much that she was desperately thirsty, and her head ached. She threw on some clothes, and opened her bedroom door quietly. Ethan had gone out to play football, and Mom and Dad were in the yard, looking at the rickety old shed. She

177

could creep down and grab a glass of juice without having to talk to anyone.

Upstairs in her room it had been terribly difficult to tell herself she didn't want a kitten. Downstairs in the kitchen, with Sky staring at her with huge, confused, sad blue eyes, it was completely impossible. Lucy held out for as long as it took to go to the fridge and pour her juice, and drink a few thirsty gulps. But the sight of Sky lost in her too-big basket was irresistible. Lucy put the glass on the table and knelt down beside Sky.

"You don't know what's going on, do you?" she asked gently. "I'm not trying to be mean, honestly," she sighed.

Sky just wanted someone to play with her. She stood up, stretched, and put a paw on Lucy's knee. She gazed at her, her head to one side questioningly. "Maaa?" she meowed pleadingly. Lucy's mom had left a cat toy in the basket, a little jingly ball with ribbons attached to it, and Sky pawed at it hopefully.

Lucy shook her head, smiling. "Okay. When it's just you and me, I'll play. But we have to pretend, all right? When Mom and Dad are around, I won't be able to play at all." She looked at Sky. She knew a kitten wouldn't understand that sort of thing, even if she did look very intelligent.

Sky batted at the ball again. Enough talking. She wanted to play.

Lucy danced the ribbons in front of Sky, bouncing the little ball up and down, and sending Sky in crazy,

179

skittering circles all over the kitchen. It was so funny! Lucy hadn't known Nutmeg and Ginger when they were kittens, and she hadn't realized how much more playful a little kitten would be than her two middle-aged, rather plump cat friends. Sky danced, she jumped, she tumbled over and over, attacking the fierce ribbons. "Oh, Sky!"

Lucy giggled.

Then she heard voices coming up the path. Mom and Dad! Quickly, she stood up and dropped the jingly ball back into Sky's basket. Sky watched her, puzzled. Was this a new game? Was she supposed to jump into the basket and pull it out again? She dived in, and popped up with a mouthful of ribbons. But Lucy had turned away. She was standing by the table, drinking her juice. Sky waited. Maybe she was supposed to creep up on Lucy, and give her a surprise? Yes! It was a hunting game! She dropped the ball and leaped sneakily out of her basket. Tummy low to the ground and ears pricked with excitement, Sky crept across the kitchen floor — slowly, slowly, ready to

181

pounce on Lucy's foot!

Just then, Lucy's parents came back into the kitchen. They saw Sky standing on her hind legs, her paws on Lucy's jeans, gazing pleadingly up at her. Lucy was ignoring the kitten entirely, not even looking at her.

Lucy's mom sighed, and went to pick Sky up and pet her. Sky gave a tiny purr — it was nice to be cuddled — but she was still gazing at Lucy. She was confused. Why didn't Lucy want to play anymore? What had gone wrong? It was as though Lucy was a different person. And not a very friendly one.

Chapter Four
A Sudden Escape

By Monday morning, Sky was even more confused. Lucy gave her lots of cuddles and was wonderful to play with when they were on their own, but as soon as anyone else came into the kitchen, she would pretend that she couldn't even see Sky. It was awful. Sky couldn't help feeling that she must have done something wrong, and she was desperate to make it better. Lucy's mom was trying to keep her in the kitchen until she settled in, but Sky had other ideas. She wanted to follow Lucy everywhere. She trailed determinedly around the house after her, and tried to climb into Lucy's lap every time she sat down.

Lucy was sitting at the table eating breakfast, so she tried it again now. But Lucy gave her one quick, unhappy glance and slid her off. Sky crept back to her basket, her whiskers drooping. Ethan made a huffing noise at Lucy, as though he thought she was being mean. "Here, Sky," he muttered, holding out his hand. "Kitty, kitty."

Sky sniffed his fingers politely, but it

was Lucy she really wanted. She gave him a little purr as he tickled her ears, though. Then she looked up hopefully at Lucy one last time, but she was staring firmly at her cereal bowl.

Lucy's mom was watching them as she buttered some more toast. "We've got to be really careful not to let Sky out of the house today when our new sofa is delivered. She isn't big enough to go outside yet."

Lucy shrugged and saw her mom give her a worried look — she was obviously thinking that Lucy still hadn't changed her mind about Sky. Lucy stared into her cereal. Things were going just as she'd planned, and she'd never felt so miserable.

School seemed even worse on Monday. A few times during class Lucy glanced at the red-haired girl, hoping she would look back, but she never did. It would be so good to have *someone* to talk to, and the red-haired girl — Lucy was pretty sure her name was Izzy — had seemed friendly before.

186

At dismissal Lucy trailed silently down the road after her mom.

"Did you meet anyone nice today?" her mom asked cheerfully.

"No," Lucy sighed. "There *isn't* anyone nice."

"Oh." Her mom looked upset, and Lucy felt a bit guilty.

Lucy glared at the new house as they turned onto their road. Then she grinned. Sky was perched on the back of the new sofa in the front room, peering out. Lucy blew her a kiss as Mom fumbled for her keys, and Sky made a flying leap off the sofa. Eventually, Lucy's mom opened the door, and Sky shot out….

"Oh, catch her, Lucy! We can't let her go into the road!"

Lucy tried to grab the kitten, but Sky was too fast for her. Sky danced around all over the yard, enjoying the game of chase. She hadn't had any time with Lucy today, and now Lucy was giving her lots of attention! She hid behind a large plant, her tail swishing excitedly, waiting to jump out.

"Sky! Here, kitty, kitty…." Lucy was creeping closer. She could see Sky's whiskers twitching from behind those big leaves. She jumped behind the plant and her hands closed on nothing as Sky clambered onto the wall.

"I'll go and get some cat treats," Lucy's mom said. "Just try to keep her in the yard, Lucy, please!"

"Oh, Sky," Lucy whispered, as Mom disappeared into the house. "I know I haven't been very nice, but don't run off, please. Come on...."

Sky stretched out to sniff Lucy's fingers as Lucy slowly moved closer. Lucy's eyes were bright and wet, and she looked so sad. Sky rubbed her head against Lucy's hand, hoping to cheer her up, and Lucy smiled a little.

"You're so beautiful," Lucy said, as she scooped the kitten off the wall and into her arms. She brushed her cheek against Sky's face, and Sky purred happily.

Gazing down the road, Lucy blinked in surprise. There was Izzy! Turning the corner, with a bigger girl who had the same red hair. They looked so alike, they had to be sisters. Did Izzy live on this road, too? Lucy watched hopefully as the two girls walked along the road, and stopped at a house a couple of doors down. Izzy suddenly looked around and caught Lucy's eye, and Lucy blushed, embarrassed to be caught staring.

Izzy gave Lucy a quick smile and a tiny wave, almost as though she were shy, too. Then she followed her sister up the path.

Lucy held Sky close, imagining how great it would be to have a friend living just across the road. They could walk to school together. Maybe have sleepovers at each other's houses. She'd always gone by car to her old school, and none of her friends lived anywhere close, not even Ellie. Without thinking, she rubbed Sky gently behind the ears, making her close her eyes and purr with delight.

"So you caught her, then?" Lucy's mom was now standing right beside her, holding a packet of cat treats, and smiling.

191

Lucy looked up, still lost in her thoughts. Then she remembered. Ellie was her friend, not Izzy. She didn't want a kitten to make her forget. She didn't want a kitten at all. She'd told her parents that…. She stuffed Sky into Mom's arms, and dashed into the house.

But she could hear Sky meowing, and she longed to rush back and cuddle her again….

Chapter Five
Secret Cuddles

Lucy was staring gloomily at the bean plants in the school garden, and wondering why they bothered growing beans when nobody liked them. Suddenly, somebody tapped her on the shoulder and she jumped.

Izzy grinned at her. "Sorry to scare you. I guess you didn't hear me coming up behind you!"

"Um, no…," Lucy replied.

"I'm Izzy. Do you live on our road, Honey Creek Road? I saw you yesterday on the way home from school." Izzy stared eagerly at Lucy.

Lucy nodded. "Yes, we just moved there," she said quietly.

Izzy didn't seem too bothered by Lucy's flat tone of voice. "That's great. There's no one else my age on our road — well, only Sean Peters, and he's worse than no one. It'll be really good to have another girl around."

Lucy smiled. It felt so nice to be wanted!

"So is that beautiful kitten yours? Is she a Siamese? Have you had her long? You're so lucky, having a kitten!"

Lucy said nothing. She didn't know

what to say. Sky was her kitten, but she wasn't going to be keeping her, was she?

Lucy stared at the ground. There was an uncomfortable silence. Izzy turned to go.

"Olivia said you were stuck-up," she said. "I told her you might just be shy, but maybe she was right." She shrugged, and marched off across the yard.

Lucy stared after her, her thoughts racing. Izzy was really nice, and seemed to want to be friends. But now she thought that Lucy was stuck-up. As Izzy opened the gate, Lucy dashed after her, trampling most of a row of carrot plants in her rush to catch her up. She caught hold of Izzy's sleeve.

"I'm really sorry. I'm not stuck-up, honestly. I just didn't know what to say." She sighed.

Izzy just looked at her. It wasn't a very encouraging start, but Lucy took a deep breath and began to explain.

"Look, I *really* didn't want to move here. We had to because of my dad's job. I just kept hoping and hoping that my mom and dad were going to change their minds. It's not that I don't think Honey Creek Road is nice," she added quickly, not wanting to be rude about Izzy's home. "And I guess this is probably a nice school, but I'm really missing my old school, and it's just not the same."

Lucy stopped for breath. Izzy looked curious, so she kept going. "Mom and Dad are trying to persuade me to like it here. They gave me Sky on Saturday, to make me feel better about the move. That's what Mom said." Lucy's eyes filled with tears. "She's supposed to help me forget my old house and my friends and everything."

197

"Wow," Izzy muttered. "I suppose I'd be miserable if I had to move somewhere totally new."

Lucy nodded.

"But at least you've got Sky. She's beautiful!" Izzy smiled.

"She is," Lucy agreed. "You're going to think I'm silly. But — well, I'm pretending I don't like her. That's why I just didn't know what to say when you asked if she was my kitten."

Izzy looked confused. "But why?"

"If Mom and Dad see I really love Sky, they'll think I've stopped missing home and I don't mind staying here," Lucy explained. It *did* sound silly. She blushed miserably.

"I *guess* that makes sense," Izzy said

198

rather doubtfully. "So your mom and dad think you don't want her?"

"Whenever they're around I don't play with Sky, or even look at her," Lucy admitted.

Izzy nodded slowly. "But ... what's going to happen? If your parents think you don't want her, won't they give her back? You're going to let them?"

"Yes. I mean, I thought I was. I was missing home so much." Lucy sat down on the bench by the gate, and heaved a huge sigh. "Only now I'm not sure I can!"

"Mmmm." Izzy sat down next to her. "I can't imagine giving her back. She's so cute!"

Lucy smiled. "She is, isn't she?" Then she put her chin in her hands and sighed again. "But I can't just change my mind now…."

"You might end up having to stay here, *and* not having a beautiful kitten," Izzy pointed out.

"I know," Lucy said gloomily.

That night, Lucy waited until her parents were both in the living room, and then crept out of bed. She stole quietly down the stairs, not wanting Ethan to hear her, either, and along the hallway to the kitchen.

Sky looked up hopefully as she opened the kitchen door. Lucy had petted her quickly a few times that evening when no one was looking.

She did wish that Lucy would be nice like that all the time. Sky waited anxiously. Was Lucy going to ignore her again?

Lucy came and sat down next to her basket, and gently petted the top of Sky's silky head. "Izzy thinks I'm silly for not telling Mom and Dad how much I like you," she told the kitten. "She said she doesn't know how I can pretend. I'm not sure I know, either," she added sadly.

Sky climbed out of her basket and clambered up Lucy's leg. She stood on Lucy's lap and butted her chin. That was sure to make her feel better. She licked Lucy, too, just to be certain. There.

Lucy giggled. "Oh, Sky, your tongue's really rough!"

Sky purred as she heard Lucy laughing. It had worked. Lucy was feeling better. She'd seemed so sad before, but now she felt warm and friendly. Sky curled herself into a comfortable ball on Lucy's knee, gave a huge yawn, and went to sleep.

Chapter Six
Making Friends

Sky woke up and yawned, stretching her paws lazily. Then she opened her eyes wide, remembering where she was. Lucy's house. The thought of Lucy made her sit up eagerly. Lucy! Where was she? Last night Lucy had cuddled her to sleep on her knee — but now she was back in her basket. Sky hopped out and went to sniff at the kitchen door. She looked up at the handle thoughtfully. Her mom could jump and open door handles, but Sky wasn't big enough yet. She prowled up and down impatiently. Maybe Lucy would be down soon, and she'd have someone to play with.

When Lucy's mom came downstairs, Sky wove around her feet, almost tripping her up, but Lucy's mom just laughed. "Are you starving, Sky? Poor kitten! Here you go." She placed a full bowl of kitten food on the floor, and Sky settled down to eat it, keeping one eye on the door.

When Lucy finally came into the kitchen, Sky danced over to her delightedly. *Where were you? I've been waiting for you! Cuddle me!* she meowed.

Lucy gulped. She cast one quick glance at Sky, her tail pointing excitedly straight up, her whiskers twitching with happiness, and then dragged her eyes away. It was so unfair to keep doing this! Sky didn't understand that she could only love her when no one was around. *Soon*, Lucy thought sadly, *Sky's going to give up on me....*

Lucy's parents watched as the kitten pawed eagerly at Lucy's leg, and Lucy ignored her again. Lucy's dad gave her mom a serious look and shook his head.

Sky gazed up at Lucy. After last night, she'd been sure that Lucy wouldn't act all strange and cold again. Her tail hung low now as she slunk miserably back to her basket, ignoring the rest of her food.

Lucy didn't touch her breakfast, either.

"Wow, you must be starved," Izzy said, watching Lucy munching swiftly through an apple at recess.

"Mmmm," Lucy nodded, swallowing. "Didn't eat much for breakfast."

"Well, we've got PE right after, so you'd better have this as well." She reached into her bag and pulled out a cereal bar.

Lucy gave her a grateful look. "Don't you want it?"

"No. Mom keeps giving me them, but they're yucky. You're welcome," Izzy smiled.

Lucy had looked for Izzy as soon as she got into school that morning, hoping that she would be there already. She'd been delighted when Izzy had seen her and rushed over. When they got into the classroom, Izzy had asked if she wanted to sit next to her — there was room, and she said Mrs. Walker wouldn't mind. Olivia and Katie looked surprised, but they didn't say anything.

"Hello," Lucy muttered shyly, as she went past. It was the first thing she'd said to them since her first day, and they looked a little confused.

It was amazing how different school was now that she had someone to talk to. Lucy found she actually enjoyed their PE class, which was soccer skills. Izzy was terrible, but she didn't mind and just rolled her eyes at Lucy and giggled hopelessly every time she had to run off across the field after the ball. Lucy was good at sports, and Mr. Jackson said he'd have to keep an eye on her for the school team. Lucy couldn't help feeling a bit excited.

When Lucy's mom came to pick her up she was amazed that Lucy came running across the playground to her, rather than trailing slowly out after everyone else. She was with a pretty red-haired girl who had a massive grin on her face. The red-haired girl grabbed a tall, red-haired woman, who had to be her own mom, then came to join Lucy.

"Did you ask her?" Izzy said anxiously.

Lucy shook her head. "Mom, please can I go over to Izzy's house? She lives across the road from us. Pleeeaase?"

"Oh, Lucy, that sounds great, but maybe another day," said Mom. "We haven't given Izzy's mom much notice." She smiled apologetically at the red-haired woman.

"Actually, it's fine by me," Izzy's mom replied. "Izzy mentioned last night that she'd met Lucy, and she'd love to have her over. Since it's Wednesday, Izzy's sister Amber has choir, so I pick Izzy up. Usually the girls walk home together. You've just moved in, haven't you?"

Izzy's mom was really friendly, and as the four of them walked home she told Lucy's mom about the neighbors, and which were the nicest shops in the area.

Izzy's mom made the girls a snack, and afterward Lucy and Izzy hung out in her room. Izzy had a sleepover bed that slid out from underneath hers, and she promised to ask if Lucy could stay the night soon.

"Amber has a portable DVD player. I bet she'd lend it to us for the night," Izzy told her.

Izzy also had a secret stash of chocolate left over from her birthday, and somehow, munching happily and chatting about the worst teachers at their school, Lucy forgot that she wanted to leave Fairfield. It seemed all too soon that Izzy's mom was calling up the stairs to say that Lucy's dad was here to take her home.

"See you tomorrow!" Izzy waved

cheerfully to her as she crossed the road. "Hey, ask your mom if you can walk to school with Amber and me!"

Lucy nodded and waved back. "I will, promise!"

Lucy walked into the kitchen, smiling happily to herself, and then stopped. Mom and Dad both had serious faces. "What is it?" she asked anxiously.

"Lucy, Mom and I have been talking. About Sky." Dad's voice was sad as he looked over at Sky's basket.

Lucy looked, too. Sky was curled up, fast asleep — she was so cute.

"We really hoped that having Sky to play with and take care of would make you feel better about the move. We know you're missing Ellie and the others." Her dad sighed. "But I'm sure you'll settle in after a while. Izzy seems very nice — it's great that you're starting to make friends."

Where is Dad going with this? Lucy gazed at her parents.

"Anyway, it looks like we made a mistake with Sky. We should have talked to you about it first, before we went ahead and brought her home."

Lucy blinked. She could see that Dad was telling her something important, but she couldn't quite seem to understand. Sky was a mistake? Lucy started to feel scared. She looked at Sky, who was still asleep in her basket, although she'd wriggled around and was now lying on her back with her paws in the air. She looked like a toy kitten.

Dad smiled sadly as Sky let out a sleepy half-meow, half-purr. "Luckily the breeder we got Sky from has been very understanding. Tomorrow evening Mom will take Sky back."

Chapter Seven
A Place to Hide

Lucy suddenly felt cold. It was just like Izzy had said. *You might end up having to stay here, and not having a beautiful kitten.*

"Oh, Lucy, don't look like that!" Her mom came over and gave her a hug. "We're not angry with you. It was our fault for not talking it over with you first."

No, you don't understand! Lucy wanted to cry out. *Don't give her back! I want to keep her!* But her voice seemed to stick in her throat as her parents went on talking.

Mom stroked Lucy's hair sadly. "Sky deserves a home where she's really wanted. She's such a loving little kitten — she needs someone to give her lots of love back."

Lucy had been about to try to explain, but that made her stop. It was so true. Sky did need a home where she was loved. Lucy had a horrible feeling that that special home wasn't here with her. She'd been so mean — Sky didn't know whether Lucy loved her or hated her. *Maybe I just don't deserve to have a kitten,* she thought.

But she had to say good-bye to Sky properly. Even if Sky didn't understand.

Later, Lucy crept downstairs while her parents were in the living room. Sky was in the kitchen, as she usually was at night, and Lucy opened the door quietly.

Sky saw her from her basket. She laid her ears slightly back, and stared up as Lucy came closer in the faint light from the hallway.

Lucy gulped. It was obvious that Sky didn't know what was going on. She crouched down by the basket. "Mom and Dad are right," she whispered to the kitten, running one finger down Sky's back. "You do deserve a better home than this. I've come to say good-bye," she said, her eyes filling with tears. One of them dripped onto Sky's nose, making her jump.

"Mrow!" she meowed indignantly, and Lucy laughed and cried at the same time, stifling the strange noise in case her parents heard. Sky's face was so funny, her blue eyes round and startled.

"Shhh, Sky!" Lucy scooped Sky up, tucking her into her robe. "Come on," she whispered. Lucy looked around quickly as she opened the kitchen door, then scurried up the stairs to her room.

Sky snuggled against Lucy's pajamas, watching curiously as they went upstairs. She'd never gotten this far before; the stairs were steep and someone always caught her before she'd struggled up more than a few steps.

Where was she going? Sky purred excitedly as Lucy opened the door to her room and placed her down gently on the floor.

Lucy snuggled under her comforter and watched Sky exploring her bedroom, sniffing her way around the boxes. Having Sky in her room made the little kitten seem much more *hers*, somehow. Lucy could imagine doing her homework up here, with Sky sitting on her windowsill watching the birds, or snoozing on her bed. Sky clambered onto the bed next to Lucy and purred lovingly in her ear.

"What am I going to do, Sky?" Lucy whispered sleepily, petting her. All of a sudden she was so tired. "I wish you could tell me what to do...."

Lucy awoke to find Sky licking her face with her rough little tongue.

"Hey, Sky…. That's a nice way to be woken up," she muttered sleepily. "I suppose you want breakfast," she said, as Sky jumped down off the bed and padded over to the bedroom door.

Lucy threw on her robe and carried Sky downstairs. When they got to the kitchen she jumped down and stared demandingly at her food bowl. "Mw-wowl!" she told Lucy firmly.

Lucy grabbed the bag of kitten food from the cupboard. She poured some into Sky's bowl, and got herself some juice from the fridge. Watching Sky busily devouring her breakfast, Lucy wondered if she could bear to let Sky go. She was so pretty! If she told her parents she'd changed her mind, maybe they could keep her....

Her mom came down a few minutes later. "You fed Sky!" she said in surprise. Then she looked at the bag that Lucy had left on the counter. "I suppose I might as well take that to the breeder's with me later. They'll be able to use it, or give it to her new owner. The basket and things, too, probably," Mom sighed.

Lucy walked quickly out of the kitchen, before she started to cry. Sky's new owner! The person who was going to really love her.... Everything was so complicated. Lucy felt like she didn't even know what she wanted anymore.

The doorbell rang. Izzy and Amber had come to pick her up for school like they'd arranged last night. Sky peeked around the front door, and Izzy nudged Amber. "Look, isn't she beautiful? Isn't Lucy lucky?"

Amber smiled. "Oh! She's so tiny. You really *are* lucky, Lucy!"

Lucy didn't want to explain what had happened in case she started crying again. "Mmmm!" she said, forcing a smile.

As soon as Amber left them at the school gates to go on to her high school, Lucy burst out, "They're taking Sky back!"

"What?" Izzy yelped. "When?"

"Today," Lucy said miserably. "Mom and Dad told me when I got home from your house last night. They said they'd made a mistake, but the people who bred Sky will take her back. Luckily." She sniffed.

Izzy gazed at her in horror. "And you're just going to let them?"

Lucy stared down, noticing that her school skirt had white hairs on it. "I suppose so," she muttered. She was crying *again*!

"You just can't!" Izzy said. "That beautiful kitten, the best present *ever*, and you're letting them take her away!" Izzy's eyes were flashing, and people were staring at them as they walked along the hallway to their classroom.

"You don't understand!" Lucy wailed.

"No, I don't." Izzy dumped her bag on their table.

"Last night I was going to tell them I'd changed my mind about Sky and wanted to keep her," Lucy explained. "I was trying to think about how to do it while I was at your house. But when I got home, they told me they were going to give Sky back because she needed someone who'd really love her. And they're right! All I've done is make her sad…," she sobbed.

Izzy made a disbelieving noise and put her arm around Lucy. "She didn't look sad the other day when you were cuddling her in your yard! She looked really happy!"

Lucy looked up at her hopefully. "Do you think so?"

Izzy thought for a moment. "Do you think maybe you've been upset about moving for so long that you're just looking on the wrong side of everything?" she asked.

Lucy felt hurt. It sounded as though Izzy thought she was just being silly.

"I'm not trying to be mean," Izzy

added hurriedly. "It's just I thought you were actually starting to like being here. You don't *really* hate it, do you?"

Lucy shook her head slowly. "Noooo," she replied. She looked up at Izzy, feeling confused. She'd been telling herself she hated Fairfield for so long, it was hard to admit to someone else that it actually wasn't so bad. "No. Since I made friends with you, it's been fun," she said, smiling. She sat down slowly on the edge of the table, thinking aloud. "And if I could keep Sky, and not have to pretend I didn't like her, it would be even better." Lucy looked shyly up at her friend — Izzy really *was* her friend. "All I have to do is explain to Mom and Dad, and everything will be okay."

Back at Lucy's house, Mom was in the hall searching for her keys, ready to go out shopping. She just had time before Lucy and Ethan came back from school. Mom grabbed her coat from the closet. "Where have I put them, kitty?" she muttered to Sky. "Oh, there they are, in my pocket all the time!" She sighed, looking at Sky's bright, interested eyes. "I'm going to miss you. But I suppose it's for the best. I'll see you in a while, little one."

Feeling lonely, Sky watched her walk down the road from her perch on the back of the sofa. Then she wandered through the house, looking for something fun to do. She could hear the washing machine rumbling in the kitchen. It would be going around and around! She liked to watch it, so she nudged the door open.

Sky didn't use her basket much during the day — she usually slept on the sofa — so Lucy's mom had put it away with her food bowl and the bag of food. It was all piled up on the counter, ready to take back that evening. Forgetting about the washing machine, Sky looked at the place where her basket was supposed to be, feeling confused. What was going on? Her bowl, her basket, all that food? Didn't they want her anymore?

But she liked it here, and she was sure Lucy was beginning to like having her here, too. Determinedly, Sky stalked out of the kitchen. This was her home now, here with Lucy!

Distracted by losing her keys, Lucy's mom hadn't closed the closet door all the way. Sky had never seen this door open before, not even a crack, and she nudged it further open with her nose.

It was full of boots and bike helmets and coats, and it looked dark and curious. Sky wriggled through the door, and wove herself between the boots to get further in. At the back was a big wicker basket, full of scarves and hats. Sky climbed into it, and burrowed under Lucy's pink, fluffy hat. Perfect. Now she would stay here until they changed their minds.

Chapter Eight
Home at Last

Lucy and Izzy had agreed to race home after school as fast as they could get Amber to go. As they dashed down their road, Lucy spotted her mom in the driveway, carrying something bulky. It looked awfully like the special box that Sky had come in.

A horrible thought suddenly struck her. What if Mom had taken Sky back earlier than planned? What if Sky was already gone?

She sped ahead of Amber and Izzy, and flung herself through the gates. Her mom had put the box down on the driveway while she closed the garage door, and it was open at the top, its flaps not folded together. It was empty.

Lucy knelt down beside it and looked in, knowing it was no use, but hoping that somehow Sky was there after all. But there was no kitten. Lucy was too late. Holding the flaps of the box, Lucy started to cry.

"Lucy!" Her mom was staring at her in horror. "Lucy, what is it? What's the matter?"

Lucy was crying too hard to speak.

Izzy and Amber had now caught up with her. Izzy stared down at the box. "Oh, no! She's gone already?"

Lucy nodded, her shoulders heaving.

"Girls, what is going on?" Lucy's mom asked.

Izzy looked up at her. "Lucy was going to tell you she didn't want to give Sky back after all. It was all a big mistake."

Lucy's mom gasped. "Lucy? Is this true?" She bent down and pulled Lucy up, putting an arm around her. Lucy clung on to her, still crying quietly.

"Yes," she gulped. "I'm sorry!"

"But why didn't you say something?" her mom asked, confused.

Lucy heaved a shuddering sigh.

"Because I thought you only gave me Sky to make me forget about everyone back home, and I didn't want to forget my friends!"

"That's not why we gave you Sky!" Her mom sounded hurt. "Although … I suppose I can understand how you'd see it like that. Oh, Lucy."

"And now it's too late, anyway," Lucy sniffed.

Her mom smiled. "Actually it's not."

Lucy looked up at her in sudden hope. "Can we get Sky back?"

"We don't have to. I was just getting the box out of the garage, that's all. Sky's inside somewhere. I'm not sure where. I've only been back 10 minutes." Lucy's mom smiled as Lucy, Izzy, and Amber dashed over to the front door. "Would you like me to let you in, by any chance?"

The girls burst into the house as soon as she opened the door, calling eagerly for Sky, expecting her to come running. Lucy couldn't help thinking how wonderful it was not to have to pretend she didn't care about her beautiful kitten. Her kitten! Sky really was hers now!

"Have you found her?" Lucy's mom called a couple of minutes later, once she'd put the box away. "I'd better call the breeder and tell her we're not bringing Sky back after all."

But Lucy, Izzy, and Amber were coming down the stairs, looking worried.

"What's the matter?" Lucy's mom asked, putting her coat away.

"She's not here," Lucy said anxiously. "She couldn't have gotten out, could she, Mom? She's disappeared. We've looked everywhere."

Her mom shut the closet door. "I don't see how she could've gotten out. She was definitely in when I left; I saw her sitting on the back of the sofa as I went out. Come on, let's look again. She's probably hiding, and playing a game with us."

But they looked and looked, and when Ethan got home he joined in, too, and Lucy's dad a while later. By the time Amber had to drag Izzy home for dinner, they still hadn't found her. Sky had disappeared completely.

Tucked away in her warm little nest, Sky had heard everyone searching and calling. She'd almost come out, but maybe they were only trying to find her so they could take her away. The voices calling her name sounded frightened and upset. She thought Lucy was crying, and that made her feel sad, too. Maybe she should come out, and make Lucy feel better. It was so hard to know.

Sky wanted her basket to go back in its place in the kitchen. If she waited until they all went to bed, maybe she could go and see if they'd put it back for her. Yes, she would come out then. She was very hungry, though, and it was a long time to wait.

Sky tunneled underneath a tasseled

scarf to make her bed more comfortable. The closet was chilly, and so lonely. Oh, she wished Lucy would come and find her — the nice Lucy who petted her so lovingly, and told her how beautiful she was. That Lucy didn't want to give her away, she was sure!

"Lucy, I know you want to keep looking, but it's really late. You have to go to bed — you've got school in the morning. We'll search outside tomorrow, even though I still don't see how Sky could've gotten out." Lucy's mom looked anxiously out the window into the darkness.

Lucy stared out the window as well, and shivered. It was so dark and cold now. Sky had only been outside the house that one time when she'd slipped through the front door. She couldn't stop imagining poor little Sky out there on her own, perhaps hiding under a bush, cold and frightened.

She hugged her mom sadly, then slowly climbed the stairs to her room. Was it only this morning that Sky had woken her up by licking her face? It seemed so long ago. She got into bed, and lay there wishing she hadn't been so silly. If only she'd told her parents sooner that she'd changed her mind, then maybe this wouldn't have happened.

Sky was determined to wait until everyone had gone to bed before she came out. Then she would go and see if they had put her things back in their proper places. If they hadn't, well, she would go back into the closet until they did! But she would find something to eat first.

As the noise in the house died down, she cautiously crawled out of her woolly nest and perched at the edge of the basket, her paws on the rim, listening carefully. Could she sneak out and look around yet? Was it safe? Maybe she could creep up the stairs and see Lucy, too. She missed her so much!

Sky threaded her way carefully across the closet, avoiding a pile of umbrellas, and squeaking with disgust as she bumped into Ethan's muddy football cleats. Here was the door — she could see a line of light shining from the hallway.

But shouldn't that line be bigger?

Sky was horrified as she realized that the door to the closet was closed. Confused, she scratched desperately at the wood, hoping to make the door open again. This door had definitely been open before. Why was it shut now? She yowled in frustration and fury, her tiny claws leaving long scratches in the paint.

Eventually, Sky's howls turned to frightened cries. She was trapped. She couldn't get out. What if she *never* got out?

Lucy! Come and find me! Please! she meowed.

But everyone else in the house was asleep, tired from searching and crying and worrying, and no one heard.

Eventually, Sky clambered back into her safe little nest. She wriggled under Lucy's hat and fell asleep, her paws sore from scratching.

A little later Lucy woke up with a start. She'd been half-dreaming, half-worrying. What if Sky hadn't just slipped out because she spotted an open door? What if she'd run away on purpose?

Lucy knew she had been behaving oddly, playing with Sky one minute, and ignoring her the next. Maybe Sky had given up on her. After all, she had been taken away from her home and her mom, too, and everything had been different and strange, just like it had been for Lucy.

I drove her away, Lucy thought miserably, certain now that this was what had happened. Suddenly she threw back her comforter. "I made her go, and it's up to me to go and find her," she muttered to herself. "I can't leave her out there thinking I don't love her. This is all my fault."

It was past midnight, and Lucy was pretty sure everyone was asleep. She grabbed her flashlight, which luckily was on top of one of her boxes, and sneaked down the stairs. She wasn't going to bother getting dressed — her pajamas were fleecy and warm. She'd just put on her nice warm robe and her fluffy hat and scarf. She was pretty sure Mom had unpacked them, and they were in that closet next to the stairs.

Inside the closet, Sky was in a restless half-sleep. Then all at once the door opened, and a beam of light cut into the gloom of the cupboard, dazzling Sky for a moment before her eyes adjusted. It was Lucy! Sky was about to run to her, when she remembered the way her basket and food bowl were piled up on the kitchen counter. Did Lucy still want her? She peered out from under Lucy's hat, her eyes big and round and hopeful in the dark.

"It's my fault," Lucy whispered to herself. "Poor Sky. All because I was so stubborn."

Sky heard her name, and Lucy's sad voice. But what did it mean?

Lucy spotted the basket, and cast the flashlight over the top, looking for her hat and scarf. It was cold outside and she might be out searching for a while — she wasn't coming back until she'd found Sky and brought her home!

Then she stopped with a gasp. Peering out from under her hat was a tiny creamy-white head. Big blue eyes blinked at her uncertainly.

"Sky!" Lucy breathed. "There you are! Mom was right! You didn't get out after all! Oh, Sky, we've been looking for you all night." She crouched down next to the basket, and looked closely at her. "Are you all right? Were you stuck in here? Why didn't you call?"

Sky watched Lucy warily. Her voice sounded loving, but a little sad as well. *Please don't give me back...*, she meowed. *I want to stay!*

"Were you hiding?" Lucy asked slowly. "Because you didn't know what was going on? Oh, Sky, I'm so sorry...." She reached out one finger, very gently, and rubbed Sky under her chin. "It's all going to be fine now, I promise. No more pretending I don't love you, because I really, really do. I know I do. Please come out!"

Sky stood up unsteadily on the pile of hats and gloves, and meowed again. *I'm so hungry!* she told Lucy.

"You must be starved," Lucy muttered. Very gently, she picked Sky up, cradling her close.

Sky could feel Lucy's heart beating as she carried her to the kitchen. Her own heart was thumping anxiously, too. Where would her basket be? She sat tensely in Lucy's arms as Lucy opened the door and turned on the kitchen light. Then she howled in dismay. It was piled up on the counter still, with her bowl and food bag. They were still going to give her away!

"Hey, hey, Sky, what's wrong?" Lucy asked. "Oh! Your basket. Does it look strange up on the counter like that? It's all right. Look." Whispering soothingly and cuddling the tiny kitten in one arm, Lucy took Sky's toys out of the basket and put it back in its warm corner by the radiator. Sky stopped crying, and leaned over Lucy's arm to sniff it suspiciously. It seemed right. Good. Now all Lucy had to do was get her food bowl.

"Lucy!" Lucy's mom was at the kitchen door, her robe half-tied, looking worried. "What are you doing?" she said. "Oh, you've found her! Where was she?" She turned to Lucy's dad, who had followed her downstairs. "Lucy found Sky!"

Lucy carried her kitten over for her mom to pet. "She was in the closet near the stairs. She must have been there all that time!" She looked seriously at her parents. "I think she was hiding because she didn't know whether we wanted her or not," she said quietly. "But we really do, don't we?"

"Of course we do," said Mom.

Her dad poured some food into Sky's bowl. "I bet she's starving."

Sky started to eat, gulping down the food, then looking hopefully for more.

"It's not that long until breakfast, Sky, don't worry!" Lucy giggled. She looked up at her mom and dad. "Can Sky sleep on my bed?" she begged.

Her mom nodded. "If you get back to bed right this minute! In fact, I think we should *all* get back to bed!"

Sky rubbed her head against Lucy's chin as she carried her upstairs. She could tell how happy Lucy was.

As Lucy snuggled up under her warm comforter, Sky curled up next to her on the pillow and purred loudly. There was no place either of them would rather be! Lucy and Sky were home.

The Abandoned Kitten

Contents

For Tabitha

Chapter One
Amy's Birthday Surprise

Amy yawned and rolled over to go back to sleep. But then she stopped halfway and bounced up in bed. It was her birthday! Was it too early to go and wake up Mom and Dad? Amy grabbed her watch off the nightstand. Six thirty. Surely that was late enough, on a birthday?

Shivering slightly in the chilly

morning, she threw on her robe and hurried down the hallway to her parents' room.

"Oh! Amy…. Happy birthday…." Her dad yawned. "Is it as early as it feels?"

"It's already six thirty," Amy replied. "Can't we get up? Please, Mom?"

Her mom was already starting to climb out of bed. "You'd better go and get dressed."

"Okay!" Amy grinned. She dashed back to her room and started to put on her school uniform, sighing a little. It was so unfair to have to go to school on her birthday. Still, since she was up early, at least Mom might let her open some of her presents….

Amy ran downstairs eagerly and burst

into the kitchen.

"Oh, wow!" she said, as she sat down at the table in front of a pile of birthday presents. She smiled as she saw that her mom had draped fairy lights around the window. "That looks beautiful!"

"Well, since you have to go to school, I thought I'd try and make breakfast special." Amy's mom put a chocolate muffin in front of her.

Just then, Dad came into the kitchen. "I hope there's one for me, too," he said, giving Amy a hug. "Happy birthday!"

"Go on, open your presents," her mom said, smiling.

Amy reached out for the nearest package, which was enticingly squashy. "Oh, it's wonderful. Grandma's so clever!" she said, as she tore off the paper and shook out a purple hoodie top, with a pink satin cat stitched onto the back, and glittery stars all around.

Her mom smiled. "I told her anything with a cat on it."

When Amy had finally unwrapped all her presents, her dad shook his head. "Do you know, anyone would think you liked cats!" he remarked, staring at the cat T-shirt, cat lunch box, kitten pencil case, and the beautiful toy Persian cat on Amy's lap. Her mom and dad knew how much she loved cats. But they just didn't think she was old enough to have one as a pet, no matter how much she begged.

"Come on, we need to get to school," Mom pointed out. "I've arranged for you to go over to Lily's today, Amy."

Amy looked up in surprise. It was the first she'd heard about this.

Her dad winked. "I need a bit of extra time to get your surprise present from us ready. Did you notice that we haven't given you anything yet? It'll be waiting for you when you get home."

"Oh, thank you!" Amy beamed at him. That sounded really exciting….

"Do you think the surprise could be a kitten?" Amy asked Lily for about the fifteenth time that day. The girls had finished their snack and had gone up to Lily's room to talk.

Her best friend sighed. "I *still* don't know! Did it sound like they'd changed their minds the last time you asked?"

Amy shook her head. "Mom said I wasn't old enough to take care of a pet. I told her you do!"

Lily smiled and petted Jewel, her big tabby cat, who was curled up on the comforter between them. "I was lucky. Mom loves cats. I didn't have to beg!"

"Dad could have needed the time to go and get a kitten." Amy was thinking aloud. "I can't think of anything else it would be. Oh, I just don't know!" She leaned down so she was nose to nose with Jewel, who stared back at her sleepily. "I wish you could tell me. Am I getting a kitten at last?"

Jewel yawned, showing all her teeth.

"Hmmm. I'm not sure what that means." Amy sighed. "Oh! Is that the doorbell?" she exclaimed, scrambling to her feet.

Lily frowned. "It's rude to be so happy about going home!" She laughed at Amy's suddenly worried face. "I'm only teasing! Get going! I've got all my fingers crossed for you! Call and tell me if it *is* a kitten!"

A few streets away, a little black kitten was sitting in a cardboard carrier, meowing sadly. She didn't like it in there, and things didn't smell right. She wanted to go back to her cozy home.

"Shhh, shhh, Jet." There was a scuffling noise at the top of the box, and the kitten looked up nervously. "Let's get you out, little one."

The kitten pressed herself into the corner as the dark box opened up. Then she gave a squeak of relief. There was her owner!

Mrs. Jones reached in and gently lifted up the little cat. She lowered herself down into an armchair, and the kitten curled up on her lap.

"Can we play with Jet, Grandma?" Two children had followed Mrs. Jones into the room. "Please!" the little girl squealed.

"Mandy, calm down!" Mrs. Jones said firmly. "You'll scare her."

The kitten looked up at the children,

both reaching out for her, and squirmed into Mrs. Jones's sweater.

"I just want to pet her," the little boy begged.

"I'm sorry, Danny. I know you both want to say hello, but she's just gotten here, and she's not really used to being with children. She'll soon settle in and then you can play with her all you want."

"Don't bother Grandma, you two. You know she needs to rest and get better." The children's mother was standing in the doorway now. "Do you want a cup of tea or anything, Mom?"

"No, no, Sarah, thank you. I'm just going to sit here with Jet to keep me company."

"Okay. Come on, you two. Don't forget to shut the door—you know we need to keep Jet in here for the next few days."

The children ran off after their mom, and the kitten relaxed. This place wasn't home, but at least Mrs. Jones was here.

"Oh, dear, it's a big change, isn't it?" Mrs. Jones tickled Jet under the chin. "Still, Sarah's right. I'm better off here where she can keep an eye on me."

273

But Jet wasn't listening. She'd tensed up again, the fur on her tiny black tail bristling. Mandy and Danny hadn't shut the door all the way, and there was another cat here. A big Siamese staring at her with round blue eyes. She meowed anxiously. Did this house already belong to another cat?

Mrs. Jones looked over at the cat. "Oh, there's Charlie. Don't worry, Jet. He's friendly; Sarah told me he'd be no trouble. No trouble at all."

"Come out into the yard!" Amy's dad held open the back door, an excited expression on his face.

"The present is outside?" Amy asked doubtfully. Why would a kitten be outside? She stepped out, and looked around at her parents, who were beaming at her.

"Look at the tree!" Dad pointed up at the big chestnut tree at the end of the yard.

"Oh! A tree house!" Amy said, sounding rather surprised.

"Don't you like it?" Her dad's voice was suddenly anxious.

"Yes, I do, I love it." Amy hugged him. It was true—she had always wanted a little private hideaway of her own. It was just that it wasn't a kitten....

"Why don't you go and check it out?" said Mom.

Amy ran across the yard and climbed the wooden ladder that her dad had fastened onto the tree trunk.

The tree house smelled wonderful, of new wood. Amy looked around it delightedly. There was a big purple beanbag to sit on, and on a tiny wooden table by the square window was a birthday cake, with pink icing.

Amy leaned out of the door, and smiled down at her parents. "It's a fabulous present. Thank you!"

"We'll cut the cake in about half an hour, okay?" said Mom, smiling.

Amy sat down on the beanbag, and sighed. She loved the tree house—but at the same time, she was secretly a little disappointed. "I should have known it wouldn't be a kitten," she whispered to herself. "It was just that I was really hoping...."

277

Chapter Two
A Curious Visitor

On Saturday it was Amy's birthday party. She and Lily and a couple of other friends from school were going to the movies, and then to her favorite restaurant to eat. She was really looking forward to it—but every so often something would remind her about kittens, and she'd feel sad again.

A Curious Visitor

"I can never decide whether to have popcorn or caramel corn," said Lily, as she and Amy walked over to the food counter. "Or do you want to share one? Amy...?" She turned to her friend. "Are you okay? You seem quiet," she whispered. "Is it about your present?"

Amy nodded. "My tree house is really cool. I can't wait for you to see it." She sighed. "Maybe they'll change their minds about my getting a cat in time for my next birthday."

Lily gave her a hug. "You can come over and play with Jewel anytime."

Amy smiled at her gratefully, but it wasn't the same as having a kitten of her own.

Mrs. Jones's daughter, Sarah, had promised her that Charlie would be fine with having another cat in the house. She was really worried about her mom, who'd had a couple of bad falls, and she wanted to be able to take care of her. And that meant her kitten, too. But Sarah just hadn't realized how jealous Charlie would be.

"Come on! Aunt Grace says she's made a cake!" The children were struggling into their coats, and Sarah was trying to hurry everyone up. It was Sunday, and they were all going over to visit Mrs. Jones's other daughter.

Jet heard the front door bang, Mrs. Jones's stick tapping as she went down the front step, and then the noise of the children growing fainter as they walked down the sidewalk. They were all going out! Jet shivered. She was hiding under a bookshelf in the living room. It was very low to the ground and she'd discovered that Charlie couldn't chase her under there, because he was too big. It wasn't a very nice place to stay—it was dusty and she had to lie flat to fit—but at least it was safe.

Now that she was allowed out of the living room and into the rest of the house, Jet spent almost the entire time hiding from Charlie. He kept pouncing on her, and he was a lot bigger than she was. They had been sharing the house for almost a week now, and he hadn't gotten any better. He kept stealing her food, too, so she was hungry all the time. But he was

281

sneaky enough only to do it when no one was looking. If the family were there, he would just glare at her until she felt too scared to eat and slunk away from her bowl.

Jet couldn't see him now, though. Maybe he'd gone out the cat flap into the yard. Nervously, she edged only her whiskers out of her hiding place and waited. She risked a paw out, then another, then squirmed forward, her heart racing. No, he wasn't there. She was safe.

She was terribly hungry, though. Charlie had chased her away from her breakfast that morning, and she really wanted to go to the kitchen and see if he'd left anything. With her whiskers trembling and her tail fluffed up, the kitten crept out into the hallway, and dashed to the kitchen door, where she did another careful search. She couldn't see him anywhere. And there was some food left! Gratefully, she scampered over to her bowl, and started to gulp down the cat food.

Behind her, on one of the kitchen chairs, hidden by the plastic tablecloth, a long chocolate-brown tail began to twitch slowly back and forth.

Jet was so absorbed in wolfing what was left of her breakfast that she didn't hear the thud as Charlie's paws hit the floor. But some sense of danger made her whiskers prickle, and she turned around just as he flung himself at her. She shot away, scooting across the kitchen floor and making a dive for the cat flap. She batted at it desperately with her nose and scrambled through, racing across the yard to hide under a bush.

Huddled against the damp leaves, she watched the cat flap swing a couple of times. Charlie wasn't following her. *Probably because he is eating the rest of my breakfast*, Jet thought miserably.

What should she do? She hadn't explored the yard much until now—

she'd always stayed close to Mrs. Jones, or hidden herself somewhere in the house. Jet poked her nose out from under the bush, sniffing the crisp morning air. It was chilly—too chilly to sit still. But she didn't want to go back inside, not with Charlie around. Instead, she set off across the yard, sniffing at the birdseed that had fallen out of the bird feeders, and cautiously inspecting the scooters and toys that the children had left lying around.

Nervously, she checked behind her to make sure Charlie hadn't sneaked through the cat flap. Just then, a fat blackbird swooped past her nose, and she pricked up her ears in astonishment. She wasn't really used to being in the yard, and birds were new and exciting.

She swished through the long grass, almost glad now that Charlie had chased her outside. The blackbird swooped and dived in and out of the plants by the fence, and the kitten trotted after it. Then it disappeared.

Surprised, she looked around, trying to figure out where it had gone. That was when she noticed the hole. There was a big gap under the fence, leading into the yard next door. This would be a perfect way to get away from Charlie. She had been looking back every so often to see that he wasn't following, but if she went into a different yard, he would never find her! Pleased with her plan, the kitten slipped underneath the fence and set off to explore.

Early that Sunday morning, Amy disappeared up into her tree house, taking the book she had to read for school. It was a chilly morning for April, so she was wearing her new hoodie from Grandma, and a pink fluffy scarf and hat. But even though it was cold, being up in the tree house felt wonderful.

It wasn't really all that high up, but it was so much fun looking down on the yards from her secret house among the leaves. The chestnut tree was at the end of their long, thin yard, but she could just see Mom moving around in the kitchen. Amy moved the beanbag so that it was in the doorway and flopped down on it, watching a blackbird hopping around in the flower bed next door. There was an early-morning mist hanging over the grass, and it felt spooky—just right for her book, which was a ghost story.

Amy read a few pages. She was just getting to a scary part when a strange rustling noise outside made her jump. A little movement by the fence caught her eye, and Amy peered down. It was a little black kitten! She was half-covered in mist, and for a second Amy wondered if this was a ghost-cat. She caught her breath in excitement, watching as the tiny thing nosed her way through the plants and spotted the blackbird, who was still pecking around in the grass on the other side of the yard.

The kitten settled into a crouch, her tail whisking from side to side, and wriggled forward onto the lawn. Amy giggled. This was no ghost! The kitten was so funny, stalking across the grass like a tiny panther. The bird spotted her at once, hopping up onto the fence and squawking angrily.

The kitten turned away and began to play with a leaf instead, as though she'd never even thought of chasing the bird.

Amy was just wondering whether, if she climbed down quietly, the kitten would let her pet it, when the little creature suddenly darted back the way she'd come—under the fence and into the mists of the yard next door.

Amy watched the shadowy little figure disappear. "I wonder who she belongs to," she whispered to herself. "And what her name is. If I could get close enough, I could look on her collar, maybe." Then she frowned. "No, I don't think she had one. I think I'd call her Misty." She put her chin in her hands, and imagined a little black kitten curled up on the end of her bed. "I can't wait to tell Lily about her!"

Chapter Three
A Shy Hello

"Have you seen her again?" Lily asked eagerly, and Amy smiled.

"Yesterday, just as I was going out into the yard. She was sitting on the back fence, right under the tree house. But when I got closer she ran off."

"You've seen her a few times now. Maybe she lives in one of the houses close by," Lily suggested.

Amy frowned. "She doesn't have a collar, though. I just wonder—maybe she's a stray. She never comes very close—I think she's very shy. A stray kitten could be like that, couldn't it?"

Lily nodded thoughtfully.

"And she looks so thin," Amy added. "I'm worried that she isn't getting enough food."

"Poor little thing!" Lily cried. "Kittens need to eat a lot. Or she might just be naturally skinny. Kittens can be. Oh, I wish I could see her."

"If we're lucky she might turn up when you come over on Friday," Amy said. Lily was a cat expert and might be able to think of a way she could help the kitten.

By now the little kitten was exploring the yards all along the road. She had discovered that she loved being outside—there were always new and exciting things to play with. Sometimes people left food out, too. Even if it was only stale bread meant for the birds, it was better than nothing, as Charlie was still stealing most of her meals. She'd gotten very good at scrambling up birdbaths. She wasn't as good at chasing the birds themselves—somehow they always seemed to figure out that she was coming. But she enjoyed trying.

Being outside was definitely better than being at her new house, anyway. Even when Charlie left her alone, which wasn't often, Mrs. Jones's two grandchildren were almost as bad.

They liked to play with her and pet her, which the kitten didn't mind too much. And sometimes it was fun to chase the string that they dangled in front of her nose. But they also kept trying to pick her up, which she hated, especially as they just grabbed her and hauled her along with her legs dangling, even though Mrs. Jones had explained how to hold her correctly. The kitten tried to stay out of their way.

"Kitty! Kitty, kitty, kitty! Where are you, Jet?" Mandy called.

The kitten slipped quickly under the kitchen table, but it was an obvious hiding place, and the little girl crawled underneath to be with her. Jet's tail started to twitch nervously.

Mandy was carrying a handful of

dolls' clothes, but she dropped them on the floor and grabbed the kitten around her middle.

Jet yowled, wriggling desperately to get away, but the little girl held her firmly. Mandy then grabbed a doll's jacket and started trying to put one of her paws into it. "You're going to look so pretty! Charlie's too big for all my dolls' clothes, but you're just the right size."

The kitten scratched frantically and raked her tiny claws across Mandy's hand. The little girl dropped Jet in surprise, and the kitten shot out from under the table and cowered in the corner of the kitchen, hissing furiously.

Mandy howled, staring at the red scratch across the back of her hand.

"What happened?" Sarah ran into the kitchen, and Mandy scrambled out from under the table. "Jet hurt me!" she wailed, holding out her hand.

"Jet did that?" Sarah turned to stare at the kitten. "Bad cat! You shouldn't scratch people!" She sounded really angry, and the kitten slunk guiltily out of the kitchen to find Mrs. Jones, knowing that she would understand.

Mrs. Jones was in her favorite

armchair, as usual. But Charlie was there, too. Curled up cozily on Mrs. Jones's lap, looking  as though he belonged there. Just where the kitten was meant to be.

Mrs. Jones was dozing, and she didn't see Jet, staring wide-eyed from the corner of the room. The kitten watched for only a second, and then she ran back the way she'd come, past Mandy still sobbing in the kitchen, and straight out the cat flap.

Charlie wasn't only taking her food now—he was taking Mrs. Jones, too.

Amy was up in the tree house, sitting by the door and looking out over the yard. She was drawing in the beautiful sketchbook that one of her aunts had given her for her birthday, with a set of new pencils, too. She was trying to remember exactly what that pretty little kitten had looked like. She wished she had seen her closer up— she still wasn't sure exactly what color her eyes were. She hesitated between the two greens in her new pencil box. Probably the lighter one. Smiling to herself, she finished coloring the eyes, and then wrote *Misty* in the bottom corner of the page.

Every time she went up to her tree

house, Amy watched for the kitten, but she hadn't seen her for a couple of days. Maybe she had a home after all....

It was just as Amy was admitting to herself that the kitten might not come back, that she saw her again. She was walking carefully along the fence that ran across the back of Amy's yard—almost underneath the tree house. Amy caught her breath. She watched as the little creature padded along the narrow boards of the fence, like a tightrope walker. She smiled proudly to herself, noting that she had made the kitten's eyes exactly the right color.

"Kitty, kitty, kitty…," she called, very gently and quietly.

The kitten looked up, startled. She had been watching a white butterfly and hadn't seen the girl at all. She tensed up, ready to run. This girl was calling her like Mandy had—was she going to try and dress her up in dolls' clothes?

But the girl didn't move. She was sitting up in a strange little house in a tree. Her voice was different, too. Quieter. She didn't make the kitten feel nervous, like Danny and Mandy did.

The girl moved, and the kitten stepped back, wondering if she should leap down from the fence and race across the yard to safety.

But the girl didn't try to grab her. She just perched herself on the ladder, with her arm trailing down. The kitten looked up. If she stretched, she could just brush the girl's fingers with the side of her face. She could mark the girl with her scent. Her whiskers bristled with surprise at the idea that she might make this girl belong to her. She took a step closer, and then another, so that she could sniff the girl's fingers.

Swiftly, daringly, the kitten nudged the girl's hand. Then she leaped down from the fence and dashed back across the yard.

Chapter Four
A Tasty Treat

Amy laughed delightedly to herself, as she watched the little kitten scurrying away. She could still feel the cold smudge of its nose against her hand.

"She came back!" she whispered happily to herself. She gazed down at her drawing and sighed. Misty was so much prettier in real life. Amy was sure she was a girl kitten, because she was so delicate-looking. Her fur was midnight-black and glossy, not the dull black of a drawing. She was very thin, though. Amy thought that she might even be thinner than when she'd seen her last week. If Misty was getting thinner, did that mean she didn't have an owner? Maybe she'd gotten lost—Amy couldn't imagine anyone abandoning such a beautiful kitten. How could they?

If she were a stray…. Amy played with her hair thoughtfully. She knew her mom and dad had said she was too young to take care of a cat, and that if she told them she'd found a stray kitten, they would want to take it to the cat shelter. But now she had the tree house. Her own special, secret place. A perfect little house to hide a kitten in.

Amy shook her head and sighed. It was only a silly dream. But dreaming was fun....

"Guess what happened yesterday!" said Amy to Lily, as soon as their moms had said good-bye at the school gates. She grabbed her friend's hand and towed her over to a bench in a quiet corner of the playground.

"What?" Lily asked excitedly.

"The kitten came back again and I touched her! She came walking along our back fence when I was up in the tree house. She was really shy, but she sniffed my fingers, and sort of nudged me, you know how cats do?"

Lily nodded. "Jewel does that, and it's really sweet. Oh, I'm so glad I'm coming to your house tonight. Maybe I'll see her, too!"

"The thing is, I definitely think she's gotten thinner since I last saw her." Amy sighed. "I'm really worried about her." She looked up at Lily. "Do you think I should feed her? I know she might belong to someone else, but I just don't see how she can. She's really thin."

Lily was practically bouncing up and down on the bench. "You should! You have to! But what are you going to feed her?"

Amy smiled. "When you come home

with me tonight, do you think you could ask to stop at the pet store so you can buy some cat treats for Jewel? I've brought some of my birthday money."

Lily nodded eagerly. "Of course. Jewel really likes the salmon ones, so we should get those."

Amy laughed. "I'm not sure this kitten would care about the flavor as long as it's food."

"I'll tell your mom I need a couple of extra cans of cat food, too," Lily added. "You can't just feed her treats."

"That would be terrific," Amy told her gratefully.

"I can't wait to see her—can we go up in the tree house tonight and wait to see if she comes?"

Amy nodded. "I thought maybe if I put some food out, she might smell it."

"Good idea. We definitely need to get the fishy flavors then. They stink! My mom won't buy the tuna cat food, because she says it makes her feel sick! A hungry kitten would smell it a mile away, I would think. Oh, Amy, this is so exciting." Lily gave her a hug. "It's almost like you're going to have your own cat after all!"

"She might not come," Amy said cautiously, but she hugged Lily back, unable to keep the smile off her face.

"You definitely want this kind!" Lily took a foil pouch of cat snacks from the shelf. "They smell really strong. The kitten won't be able to resist them." She placed the cat treats in her basket. "I just thought of something. You'll have to give her a name. What are you going to call her?"

"I named her the first time I saw her," Amy admitted. "Her name is Misty, because I saw her coming toward me out of the mist." She picked up a different packet of cat treats and added them to Lily's basket.

"Let's get these, too—if this cat on the front were a kitten, it would look exactly like Misty."

"Very, very cute," Lily said.

"She is." Amy nodded. "I really hope she comes back this afternoon so you can see her! Oh, look, Mom's waving at us to hurry up." Amy's mom was waiting outside the pet store for them.

"Oh, my, you needed a lot of cat food!" she said to Lily as the girls came out of the store.

Lily giggled. "Jewel is very greedy," she said, winking at Amy, or trying to; she wasn't very good at it, and had to screw up her face.

"Lily, are you all right?" Amy's mom asked. "Is there something in your eye?"

Amy burst out laughing, and her mom shook her head. "You two— sometimes I think it's a good thing I don't know what you're up to."

Amy and Lily grinned at each other. Secrets were so much fun—and this was definitely the best one they had ever had.

They sneaked the cat food out into the yard while Amy's mom was getting a snack ready for them.

"Wow!" Lily looked up at the tree house. "Your dad built that? He's amazing!"

"It's cool, isn't it?" Amy agreed.

Lily hauled herself up the ladder and gazed around the inside of the tree house, admiring the bookshelf and the big purple beanbag.

"Come on, let's open these." Amy tore at the foil packet of cat treats eagerly. "I thought we could spread them out along the branch that almost touches the fence. I'm pretty sure Misty could jump onto it."

Amy carefully leaned out the doorway to sprinkle some cat treats onto the wide branch below. "Now we need to wait," she said, edging backward. She emptied the rest of the packet in the doorway just in front of her, then sat hugging her knees and staring over the yards, searching for a little black figure.

Amy and Lily had meant to be totally silent, so that they wouldn't scare away the kitten, but they couldn't resist chatting. They were deep in a discussion of exactly why Luke Armstrong in Mrs. Dale's class was so mean when Amy suddenly clutched Lily's arm.

"Look!" she ordered, in a hissing whisper.

"Oh!" Lily gave a little squeak of excitement. "Is that her?"

"I think so." Amy leaned out to look further along the fence, where a black shadow was clambering over the ivy branches. "Yes, it's her! Oh, I hope she can smell the cat treats."

Scrambling through the leaves, her paws slipping on the thin branches, the kitten certainly could. She was terribly hungry. Charlie was still stealing all her food, and no one seemed to notice— Sarah was always busy, and Mrs. Jones wasn't very well and was spending most of her time resting in her chair. Quite often she had Charlie sitting on her now, and she would pet him, while the kitten watched miserably from under the sofa, or peeking out from under the bookcase.

But now she could smell something tangy and delicious, and her stomach was making little rumbling noises. She trotted eagerly along the fence. Oh, the smell was getting even stronger!

The kitten stopped suddenly and

wobbled on the fence. She was there—
the girl from yesterday! And there
was another one with her. The kitten
watched them warily.

Then the girl
she'd seen before
held out a little
packet, and tipped
something out
of it, and
the kitten knew
that was where
the wonderful
smell was
coming from.
The tip of her
little pink tongue
stuck out—she
was so hungry.

Amy couldn't help giggling. The kitten was so cute, with her tongue just poking out like that. It made her look really silly.

The kitten put her front paws up on the tree branch, and the girls exchanged excited glances. Then she jumped all the way up, and found the first cat treat. She crunched it up in seconds, and scampered forward, sniffing for more. When she got to the end of the branch, after about six more treats, she stopped and looked anxiously at Amy and Lily. She could see—and smell—the big pile of treats just in front of them.

Amy sighed. "Maybe she's too frightened to come closer," she whispered.

Suddenly, the kitten sprung up onto

the tree house ladder, and Amy and Lily held their breath. Then, keeping one eye on the girls, she started to gobble up the treats from the doorway.

When they were all gone, she licked the place where they'd been, then looked up hopefully.

"She's still hungry!" Amy said. "Let's open another packet."

Lily shook her head. "No way. She'll be sick. A whole packet is a lot more than she should have, anyway!"

Amy nodded. Then she held out one hand, very slowly, to the kitten, who was staring at her seriously. Amy scratched her gently behind the ears, and she half-closed her eyes with pleasure.

"Hello, Misty," Amy whispered.

Chapter Five
The Tree House Sleepover

The kitten sat there a little nervously, still ready to run, as Amy petted her and then Lily joined in, too.

"Isn't she beautiful?" Amy said proudly.

"The prettiest kitten I've ever seen—except Jewel," Lily added, out of loyalty. "Oh, Amy, she's purring!"

She was. Amy had just found the

exact itchy spot behind her left ear, and the kitten had her eyes closed, and a tiny little throaty purr was making Amy's hand buzz.

"Snack time, girls!"

The kitten's eyes shot open. She leaped off the ladder and raced back along the branch, jumping down onto the fence and disappearing under a bush.

"'Bye, Misty!" Amy called after her quietly. "Why did Mom have to pick just then to call to us?" she complained to Lily as they scrambled down from the tree house. "I think Misty might even have let us pick her up."

Lily nodded. "She was definitely friendly. But you're right; she is much too thin. When I petted her, I could

318

feel her ribs. She needs a nice owner to feed her."

The kitten obviously agreed. She came back to the tree house the next afternoon at the same time, and Amy opened one of the cans of cat food she'd bought. She put it in an old plastic bowl she'd borrowed from the kitchen cupboard, and sat in the doorway of the tree house, watching Misty gobble it down. Misty let Amy pet her again, too, and even put her paws on Amy's leg, as though she were considering climbing into her lap.

"Are you going out to the tree house again?" Mom asked. "It's raining, though!

I didn't realize you loved it that much."

"It's my best present ever!" Amy giggled, a little guiltily. She *did* love the tree house, but that wasn't the main reason she was spending so much time out there. Every afternoon that week, as soon as she got home, she'd rushed right there to look out for Misty.

She threw on her hoodie over her uniform and went out to the tree house. The ladder was slippery from the rain so she climbed up slowly, peering out along the fence for a little kitten. But no kitten came running to see her today. She sighed. Maybe Misty was hiding from the rain somewhere.

She stood up and pulled open the tree house door, planning to sit and read on the beanbag, while keeping an eye out for Misty through the window.

But the beanbag was already occupied.

A little kitten—her fur shiny and spiky from the rain—was curled up on it, fast asleep.

Now that she had discovered that the tree house had a soft, comfortable place to sleep, and that Amy would come and feed her, Misty spent most of her days there, even though she still went back to Mrs Jones' house to sleep at night. She had climbed in through the half-open window that first time to get out of the rain, and Amy hadn't seemed to mind. In fact, she'd looked really pleased, and spent a long time petting her. The window was always open a little bit now, so that she could get in, and there would always be a little bowl of cat treats or something else delicious waiting for her.

"I don't know if I'm imagining it, but I think you're looking plumper,"

Amy told the kitten lovingly, a week after she'd first found her inside the tree house. She petted the little black tummy as the kitten lay sleepily in her lap. "Are you getting fatter, Misty?"

"Prrrrp." The kitten purred, and yawned. Then she snuggled up on Amy's lap, feeling more at home than she had in a long time.

Amy petted her gently, wishing Misty was really hers. "Stay here, kitty," she whispered. "This is your tree house, now, too." But it was getting dark, and Amy knew she'd have to head inside soon and leave the kitten all alone.

"Amy! Your dinner's getting cold!" came her mom's voice from just below the tree house.

Amy jumped and so did Misty, springing off her lap.

She could hear her mom climbing up the ladder. Panicking, Amy dropped her hoodie top over Misty. She couldn't let the secret out now—not when Misty felt almost hers. Mom would never let her keep a kitten.

Amy's mom poked her head in the doorway. "I've been calling you for a while now!"

"I'm sorry!" Amy got up quickly and went over to her mom, hoping she wouldn't see the wriggling hoodie behind her. She followed her down the ladder.

Misty edged her way out from under the top, shaking her fur angrily. Why had Amy done that?

She slunk over to the tree house door and watched Amy going across the yard toward the house. Misty slipped out along the branch and jumped down onto the fence, then into Amy's yard. Keeping her distance, she followed Amy, trotting after her. But just as she reached the house, Amy closed the door.

Misty stood outside it sadly. She wished she could follow Amy into the house. It looked warm and friendly.

There was a big magnolia tree, growing close to the kitchen window, and Misty scrambled up the trunk to a branch, then jumped onto the windowsill. She could see Amy, and two other people, laughing and eating.

She meowed, hoping that Amy would see her and let her in. But the man sitting closest to the window was the one who stood up and came to look.

"It's a cat!" He laughed. "A little black kitten. Come and see, Amy."

Amy jumped as she saw Misty, accidentally knocking her glass of juice off the table. It smashed on the floor, and the woman got up with a sigh.

Misty leaped back onto the branch, hiding in the gathering darkness, and watching as they cleaned up the mess. She wished she were in there with them, but Amy had seemed upset to see her and she didn't know why. Misty watched for a while, until Amy disappeared and the lights went off. Then she padded sadly across the yard and back up into the tree house. But this time she didn't sleep on the beanbag. She curled up on the hoodie top instead. It smelled like Amy.

"Mom came up to the tree house and almost saw Misty last night!" Amy told

Lily before school on Friday morning. "I had to throw my hoodie on top of her, poor thing! And then she was suddenly there at the window, and Dad saw her!" She sighed. "It's fun having a secret kitten, but I wish I didn't have to hide her all the time. It would be so nice to be able to take her inside, too. I'd love her to sleep on my bed, like Jewel does with you."

"It is nice," Lily admitted. "She keeps my toes toasty. Do you think your mom and dad really wouldn't let you keep her?"

Amy shook her head thoughtfully. "I've begged for a kitten for so long—if they were going to let me have one, wouldn't they have given in by now? I can't see them changing their minds."

"But she's so cute!"

"Maybe I should tell them about Misty. But what if they make me take her to a cat shelter?" Amy shuddered at the thought.

Even so, she couldn't stop imagining how wonderful it would be to curl up and sleep with her own little kitten. She just had to think of a way....

"This is great!" Lily said excitedly, as she laid out her sleeping bag on the floor of the tree house. "I'm so glad Mom agreed to let me stay over. Do you really think Misty will come and sleep with us, too?"

"I think she spends the night here sometimes. I tried brushing all the cat hairs off the beanbag last night, and there were more this morning. So she must have been here...."

Amy had come up with the sleepover plan at school, and the girls had begged their moms to let them do it that Saturday. Lily's mom had been a little worried that they would be cold, but she'd agreed in the end, when Lily reminded her about the special sleeping bags they'd bought to go camping. She even had a spare one for Amy!

"This is even better than camping! Oh, I hope Misty comes," Lily said excitedly.

Amy nodded, glancing over at the window from her sleeping bag. It wa too dark to see much—especially a black kitten. Misty had spent the afternoon in the tree house, but she'd run off when Amy started to move things around to get ready for the sleepover.

They chatted for a while by the light of their flashlights, but they kept yawning as it got later and later.

"I don't think she's going to come," Amy said sadly, when she looked at her watch and discovered it was 10 o'clock.

"It's okay." Lily gave her a hug. "It's a fun sleepover anyway. Maybe we'll see her in the morning."

Amy nodded, but she did feel disappointed. And as Lily yawned more and more, and then drifted off to sleep, she felt lonely, too. The wind was blowing and she could hear the creak of the branches. It seemed to shake the tree house more at night, although she didn't see why it would. Amy lay there with her flashlight, making a circle on the ceiling, worrying about Misty. Where was she on this chilly night?

A sudden thud made her yelp with fright, and she swung her flashlight around. The beam caught a pair of glowing green eyes, staring at her in surprise.

"Misty! You came!"

Purring delightedly, the kitten raced across the boards to leap onto Amy's sleeping bag, padding at it eagerly with her determined little paws.

Amy lay down again, and yawned. "I'm so glad you're here," she whispered.

Misty curled up next to Amy's shoulder, half inside the sleeping bag. It was wonderfully warm. She was very glad she was there, too.

Amy petted Misty gently, and soon the two of them were fast asleep.

Chapter Six
Mom's Discovery

"Oh, Amy, she's here!"

Amy blinked sleepily and looked over at Lily, who was sitting up in her sleeping bag. There was a warm, furry weight on her chest, and Amy remembered her late night visitor. Misty had stayed all night!

"She came by a little while after you went to sleep." Amy suddenly sat up, making Misty squeak. "Lily, what time is it? My mom! She said she'd bring us our breakfast in the morning."

Lily's eyes widened. "It feels like we slept really late." She wriggled over to the door and opened it. "Oh, no! She's coming across the yard! With toast!"

"I don't care if she has toast! What are we going to do?"

But they were both sleepy and giggly with excitement about Misty, and all Amy could think of was to pull her sleeping bag up over the kitten. Which Misty didn't like. She wriggled about indignantly, and just as Amy's mom appeared at the top of the ladder, she poked her head back out.

"Hello, girls! Did you sleep well?"

Amy's mom smiled at them. "I thought you might be hungry." Then she noticed Misty, and her eyes widened. "Amy, is that a cat?"

"It's a kitten," Amy told her, cuddling Misty close.

"Where on earth did it come from?" her mother asked, sounding confused.

"I found her," Amy said defensively. "She's a stray. I've been taking care of her."

"But she must belong to someone. Oh, Amy, I think we need to speak to your dad about this. Come back to the house, right now."

Amy climbed awkwardly down the ladder, with Misty still snuggled up against her pajamas. Misty was shivering, as if she could tell that something was wrong.

Amy's dad was drinking some tea at the table and looked up in surprise as he spotted Amy holding Misty.

"Amy, isn't that the kitten who at the window the other day?" he said, getting up to take a closer look.

Misty hissed nervously, as this big man suddenly loomed over her.

"Sorry, kitty. I didn't mean to scare you. She's a sweet little thing, isn't she?"

"But whose sweet little thing, that's the point!" Amy's mom said.

"I don't think Misty belongs to anyone, Mrs. Griffiths," Lily put in.

"She has a name? Amy, you've named her?" Amy's mom stared at them suspiciously. "This isn't just a one-time thing, is it? How long have you been keeping this kitten in your tree house?"

"I haven't been keeping her there. She just came! I first saw her a couple of weeks ago. Just after my birthday. But I don't know how often she sleeps there."

Mom turned to Lily. "All that cat food that you bought! Was that for this kitten?" she demanded.

"Y-yes," Lily admitted, looking guilty.

Mom sighed. "Amy, it's not up to you to feed somebody else's cat! We'll never get rid of her now. Not if you've been feeding her. We need to find the kitten's owner."

"She doesn't have an owner!" Amy protested.

"She must," her mom said firmly.

"Honestly, she doesn't. She's a stray. She really doesn't belong to anyone. She doesn't even have a collar. And look how thin she is!" Amy paused and looked at Misty. "Well, she isn't now, but that's only because I've been feeding her. She was so skinny, Mom! Ask Lily."

Amy's mom sank down into a chair. "I know you two are in this together," she snapped. "I can't believe you've both been hiding someone else's kitten!"

"I'm sorry, Mrs. Griffiths...," Lily muttered, and Amy put an arm around her, feeling upset. She hadn't meant to get her friend into trouble.

Amy's dad pulled up a chair and took a sip of his tea. "Okay. Let's not get upset," he said. "Sit down, girls, and tell us what happened with the kitten."

Amy sat down next to her dad. She looked up at Mom, determined to make her understand. "Misty was really nervous at first. It took a long time before she'd let me pick her up. She was really scared. Even if she did have an owner, they haven't taken care of her very well."

Misty put her paws on the table and sniffed hopefully at Dad's tea.

Dad laughed. "She looks hungry.

Should I give her some milk? Since Amy's already been feeding her, it can't make that much difference."

Amy's mom only sighed, but Amy shook her head. "No, Dad. Cats aren't supposed to drink milk. It gives them an upset stomach. You can give her some water, though. And I could go and get one of her cans of food from the tree house."

Misty meowed hopefully, and Amy's dad nodded. "She knows what you just said. Go ahead."

When Amy and Lily came back, Misty was sitting on her dad's lap.

"Dad! I didn't know you liked cats!"

"She was pretty determined." He shrugged. But he was smiling, and he petted Misty's head very gently, as though he knew exactly how to handle a kitten.

Amy watched, wide-eyed. Mom and Dad had always been so firm about her not having a cat that she'd thought they didn't like them. But Dad looked really happy having Misty on his knee. Amy stared at him hopefully, and then exchanged a thoughtful look with Lily.

Just then, Misty jumped lightly off Amy's dad's lap, stepped delicately around the table to her mom, and sat staring pleadingly up at her, her sparkling green eyes looking as big as saucers.

"She's a charmer!" Amy's dad laughed. "She wants to stay."

"Stay! We can't keep her! I can't believe you're giving in!" Amy's mom protested. "Yes, she is cute, but we said Amy was too young for a pet."

"She's been taking care of this one pretty well so far," Amy's dad pointed out. "I didn't know cats shouldn't have milk. And this is a very sweet little cat." Misty meowed hopefully at Amy's mom.

"We'd better feed her, anyway," Mom said, shaking her head. "She's obviously hungry."

Amy lifted Misty off the table and placed her on the floor, while her mom took out an old bowl. Mom opened the can of cat food and started to empty it out. Purring, Misty butted her head against her leg, making Mom laugh with surprise.

Mom shook her head. "I never thought I'd say this, but all right.

You can keep her here—for the moment. If we find out she actually belongs to someone else, she goes right back! And I'm going to call the vet, and make sure that no one's asked about a lost kitten. All right?"

Amy threw her arms around her mom. "Yes. But she doesn't have an owner, I'm sure." She then looked down at the kitten, who was digging into the food greedily. "This is your new home, Misty!"

Chapter Seven
The Lost Kitten

Over the next few days, even Amy's mom got used to the idea of having a cat. Misty was so sweet, and very well-behaved. Amy's mom had been worried about her making messes in the house, but Amy's dad went out and bought a litter box, and Misty soon showed that she was house-trained.

"I don't think she can have been born feral," Amy's mom said, tickling Misty under the chin. "She's so friendly. I'm still worried that she's somebody's pet."

Amy folded her arms and frowned. "Well, it was somebody who didn't love her as much as we do!" She sighed. "Okay, okay, Mom. I promise. We'll give her back, if anyone says they've lost her." But she was certain they wouldn't.

Misty and Amy still spent a lot of time in the tree house. It was Misty's favorite place, and Amy loved curling up there with her. But once Misty had proved she could use the litter box, she was allowed anywhere in the house, too. She loved exploring—the house was full of warm, comfortable places.

And Amy's dad was very nice to sit on. She was even allowed to sleep on Amy's bed, since she hated being shut in the kitchen. They had tried it on her first night in the house, but Misty had meowed frantically, and in the end Amy's mom had given in. Now she slept snuggled up with Amy, or sometimes blissfully curled on Amy's toes.

Amy spent the last of her birthday money buying her toys, and a collar—a pink one that looked beautiful against her black fur.

Misty could still remember her old home with Mrs. Jones, but she knew she belonged to Amy now.

Mrs. Jones sat in her armchair, staring out at the front yard, and petting Charlie. But she was frowning. "It's been a week since I've seen Jet now," she muttered to the Siamese cat. "I hadn't realized, because she was only popping in and out even before. But she hasn't even been back for her food." She looked down at Charlie worriedly. "I have to say, Charlie, you're heavier than you used to be. Have you been eating Jet's food?" She pushed him gently off her lap and stood up, leaning on her cane. Slowly, she walked into the kitchen, with Charlie trotting after her.

"Sarah, when did you last see Jet?" asked Mrs. Jones, easing herself onto a kitchen chair.

Her daughter looked surprised. "Oh. I don't know, Mom." She glanced over at the cat food bowls, both of which were empty. "Well, she's eaten her breakfast, so she must have been here this morning, although I didn't actually see her." She smiled as Charlie wove around her ankles. "It's a shame we can't ask him!"

"Hmm." Mrs. Jones frowned. "I don't think we need to ask him. It's clear exactly who's been eating Jet's food. Look how much plumper he is!"

Sarah shook her head. "Oh, no. He wouldn't!"

"Sarah, I haven't seen Jet for a week. And before then she was so flighty and scared that I'd only see her here and there for a second. I think Charlie frightened her away."

"Charlie's not like that, really...." But Sarah was looking a little worried.

"It isn't his fault," said Mrs. Jones. "This is his house, after all. But we have to find Jet. I should've realized what was going on, but those new pills Dr. Jackson gave me made me so tired. Poor Jet! She must be starving by now.

She doesn't know the area at all…. She might've gotten lost or she could even have been run over." Mrs. Jones's voice wobbled at the thought.

Sarah came over and put her arm comfortingly around her mother. "Don't worry, Mom. We'll find Jet. I'm sure she didn't go too far."

One afternoon, two weeks after their sleepover, Amy and Lily were walking back from school, chatting away as their moms followed behind.

"Dad's going to put in a cat flap this weekend," Amy told her friend happily.

But Lily didn't reply. Amy looked around and realized that Lily wasn't actually there. She'd stopped and was looking up at something stuck to the lamppost that they'd just passed.

Amy went back to see what Lily was staring at. "What is it? Oh, no...."

It was a poster, with a photo of a small kitten, and the words: "LOST. Jet, a black kitten. Please check sheds and garages in case she has been trapped inside. Contact Mrs. Sylvia Jones if you have seen our cat." Underneath there was a phone number and an address.

Amy stared at the poster numbly. "Do you—do you think it's Misty?" she whispered to Lily.

"It looks so much like her," Lily admitted sadly. "And Rosebush Way is only around the corner from you, isn't it?"

Tears welled up in Amy's eyes. "I don't want to give her back," she muttered. "It isn't fair. Misty doesn't love this Mrs. Jones, whoever she is. She can't, or she wouldn't have come to live with us. And think how thin Misty was when we first saw her—she mustn't have taken good care of her!"

Lily nodded. "What are you going to do?"

Amy looked up at the poster. "I could just pretend I haven't seen it. That Mrs. Jones doesn't deserve to have Misty back—I wouldn't feel guilty." Then she gazed at the photo of Misty again. "Well, only a little bit...."

She glanced along the road. Her mom and Lily's mom had almost caught up to them. She could just tear down the poster, then Mom would never know.... But as her mom approached, Amy could see that she was holding another copy that she must have taken from somewhere further down the street.

"Oh, Amy. You've seen it, too. I'm so sorry, but it looks like Misty has a home after all."

"But how do we know it's her?" Amy whispered.

"She does look very similar," Mom said gently.

"She didn't like her old home, or she wouldn't have run away. She's ours now. Dad was even going to put in a cat flap!"

"I know, Amy. But someone's missing her—this Mrs. Jones—"

"She doesn't deserve a kitten!" Amy sniffed, and Lily squeezed her hand.

"We have to take her back," said Mom. "Remember, it was our deal."

Amy was silent for a moment. There was nothing she could say. "I know. But I still think it's wrong."

Back home, Misty wasn't in the house, running to the door with welcoming meows, like she usually did.

"Maybe she's in the tree house," Amy suggested. But a little seed of hope was growing inside her. If she couldn't find Misty, she wouldn't have to give her back, would she?

Amy ran out into the yard and climbed up to the tree house, but it was empty. She sat down on the beanbag. It felt warm, as though Misty might have been curled up there until a moment ago. "Oh, Misty, I wish I'd kept you a secret," she whispered. "Please don't come!"

But then she heard a familiar thud on the boards of the tree house as Misty jumped from the branch. The tears spilled down Amy's cheeks as the kitten ran to her, leaping into her lap.

Misty rubbed her head lovingly

against Amy's arm, and then stood up with her paws on Amy's shoulder, and licked the wet tear trails with her rough little tongue.

"That tickles!" Amy half-laughed, half-sobbed. She picked her up gently. "I'm sorry, Misty, but we have to go and find Mom." Amy carried her down from the tree house and across the yard. Misty purred in her arms, so happily. She was such a different kitten from the nervous little creature Amy had first seen. It felt so wrong to take her back!

"Oh, you found her!" Mom came over to pet Misty as Amy opened the kitchen door. "Please don't cry, Amy." But she looked close to crying herself, as she gave Amy a hug. "I don't want to give her back either, but we have to. You know we do. Do you want to wait until tomorrow? So you can have tonight to say good-bye?"

Amy shook her head. "No. That would be worse. We should go now. Come on, Mom, please, let's just get it over with."

"All right. I'll call the number on the poster. Rosebush Way isn't far. We can just carry her there, can't we?"

Amy nodded and sat down at the table with Misty, half-listening as Mom explained to someone on the phone that they'd found their missing kitten. With shaking fingers, Amy started to take off Misty's pink collar. Misty wasn't even Misty anymore! She had another name.

"They're really glad to know she's safe," Mom told her gently. "I said we'd bring her over." She grabbed her bag, and they set out, Amy with Misty held tightly in her arms as they walked down their street and along another road, to the little cul-de-sac that was Rosebush Way.

Misty looked around her curiously, wondering what was happening. Amy had never carried her outside like this before. Then, all of a sudden, her ears went back flat against her head as she recognized where they were going. Why was Amy bringing her *here*? She struggled in Amy's arms and meowed with fright as they walked down the front sidewalk.

"Oh, Mom, she doesn't want to!" Amy protested, but her mom had already rung the doorbell.

The door opened, and an elderly lady stood there, staring at them in delight.

"Jet! It really is her! Oh, thank you so much for finding her!"

Amy only just stopped herself from shouting, "No, her name's Misty!" Instead, she stared at the brooch on the lady's sweater, which was a little silver cat with green glass eyes.

"Come in, please! Oh, Jet, where have you been?" Mrs. Jones petted Misty, and Misty actually relaxed and purred, and let the lady take her from Amy.

Amy felt the tears starting to burn the backs of her eyes again. This really was Misty's owner. It was true. Her little cat belonged to someone else.

Chapter Eight
Coming Home

Misty felt very confused. She was back with Mrs. Jones, but Amy was there, too. She wasn't sure what was happening. Mrs. Jones had Charlie now, so why had Amy brought her here? But it was so nice to have Mrs. Jones holding her again. She rubbed herself against the lady's cheek lovingly.

Mrs. Jones led them into the living

room and sat down with Misty on her lap. "Where did you find her?" she asked, smiling at them so gratefully that Amy felt guilty.

"She came into Amy's tree house," her mom explained. "We did ask around, but no one seemed to have lost a kitten. She's actually been with us a couple of weeks. I'm sorry. You must have been so worried."

Mrs. Jones nodded. "I was terrified that she'd gotten lost or had even been run over. I've just moved here to live with my daughter, so Jet doesn't know the area very well." She scratched Misty behind the ears, and the little cat stretched her paws out blissfully. "She kept wandering off—we hardly saw her—and then she disappeared. I thought she'd gone too far and gotten lost."

Mom gave Amy a look, and Amy stared at the carpet, feeling miserable and guilty. Mrs. Jones had hardly seen her because Amy had been tempting her away. She'd been so selfish! Mom had been right—she really had stolen someone else's cat.

"Amy took care of her very well," her mom said, giving Amy a hug. "We'd always thought she was too young for a pet, but we've changed our minds after watching her with your cat. We're definitely going to get a kitten of our own. I mean it," she added to Amy in a whisper. "We're so proud of you."

There was a scuffling noise at the door, and Misty suddenly tensed up. She had forgotten! It had been wonderfully quiet, almost like things used to be, with just Mrs. Jones. But now Mandy and Danny were home!

"Grandma! Grandma! Oh! You've gotten Jet back!" A little boy raced into the room and tried to grab Misty.

Amy gasped as she watched Misty cower back against Mrs. Jones. A little girl came running in after him and tried to pull her brother away so she could reach the kitten, too.

"Gently, Danny! Mandy, be careful! You'll frighten her," Mrs. Jones cried. The children stopped shoving as their mom came in. "These are my grandchildren. They've missed her, too," Mrs. Jones explained to Amy and her mom. "And this is my daughter, Sarah."

Sarah was smiling delightedly. "I'm so glad you've found her. We've all been so worried."

Amy looked anxiously at Misty—or Jet, she supposed she should call her now. She was pressed against Mrs. Jones, her ears twitching with fright. Amy thought the children were loud, so she couldn't imagine how a kitten felt.

"We'd better go—leave you all to settle down," Amy's mom said.

"Please, let me have your number—I'd like to call and let you know how Jet is. I'm really so grateful." Mrs. Jones stood up, with Jet held against her shoulder, and led them out into the hallway. "My goodness! Jet, what is it?"

The kitten suddenly scrambled her way up Mrs. Jones's shoulder and leaped to the top of a shelf, almost knocking over a vase. Her tail was fluffed up, and her ears were laid back. Charlie was here!

"Oh, you've got another cat!" Amy exclaimed, seeing the sleek Siamese padding along the hallway, staring up at her little Misty.

"Yes, that's Charlie. He belongs to

my daughter. He and Jet don't always get along too well. But I'm sure they'll settle down now that she's back."

Watching Misty spitting angrily from her safe spot on the shelf, Amy thought that it didn't look like they got along at all.

"You were very good, Amy," her mom said, as they walked home. "I really did mean it about your getting your own kitten."

"Thanks," Amy whispered. "Not for a while, though," she added. She knew she should be happy at the idea of her own kitten. But at the moment all she could think about was Misty, scared by those noisy, grabby children, and terrified of that Siamese cat. It made her want to cry. When she'd first seen Misty with Mrs. Jones, she'd thought she'd gotten it all wrong, and Misty did belong with her. But now she wasn't sure. What if that Siamese had been stealing all of Misty's food and that's how the kitten had ended up so thin? She wouldn't be surprised. She was almost sure that Charlie had made Misty run away. And now Amy had made her go back.

Misty raced across the living room, heading for her hiding place under the bookshelf. But she couldn't get in! She wriggled frantically, but she'd grown— two weeks of good food, and she was simply too big to fit into her special safe place. Why had Amy left her here? Was she going to come back? Shaking, she turned back to face Charlie, who was right on her tail. She hissed defiantly and raked her little claws across his nose. But he was just so big! With one swipe of his long brown paw he sent her rolling over and over across the carpet, and then he jumped on her.

"Honestly! Mom, she's fighting with Charlie already! Stop it! Bad cat!" Sarah tried to pull the two of them apart as they scratched and spat.

Mrs. Jones heaved herself up from her chair and tried to help. "Jet, Jet, come here. Oh, he's hurting her." She waved Charlie away with her cane and leaned down to scoop up the little kitten. "Oh, dear…." She sat down again, the kitten a ball of trembling black fur in her arms.

"Charlie hates not being able to use the cat flap; that's why he's being grumpy," Sarah muttered, picking up

Charlie and holding him as he wriggled and spat at Jet.

"I know, but Jet might run off again if we let her out. We need to keep her in for now, so she starts thinking of this as her home." Mrs. Jones petted her gently.

Sarah sighed. "We'll just have to keep them apart until they get used to each other."

Mrs. Jones looked worriedly down at the kitten, still shaking on her lap.

"Maybe I was wrong to say you'd get along with Charlie.... I suppose I was just so happy to have you back. Poor little Jet. What are we going to do with you two?"

After school a few days later, Amy was up in the tree house lying with her head resting on the beanbag. There were little black hairs on it here and there. She looked up and saw that sitting on the shelf, there was still one can of cat food left that she'd never remembered to bring into the house. It was all she had left of Misty, that and her collar, which was on her nightstand.

Mom kept mentioning the idea of

another kitten, and Lily had bought her a cat magazine so she could look at what kind of cat she might like. But Amy just couldn't think about it yet. It would feel like betraying Misty— betraying her all over again, because Amy felt sure they had done the wrong thing by taking Misty home. She kept listening for that telltale thump on the wooden boards that meant Misty was coming back to her, but it never came. She supposed Mrs. Jones was keeping Misty in the house so she didn't wander off again.

It had been five days. Almost a week. Maybe after a week, they'd let Misty go out into the yard. Maybe she'd come walking along the fence again, and Amy could at least pet her.

That wouldn't do any harm, would it? As long as Amy didn't feed her, no one could say she was trying to tempt her back. Even just seeing her would be enough. All she wanted was to know that Misty was all right.

Mom was calling her for dinner. Amy looked hopefully along the fence as she climbed down the ladder, but there was no Misty trotting along to see her.

She sat down at the kitchen table, picking at her pasta and staring at the newspaper ad that Mom had called. "Kittens, eight weeks old. Tabby and white." Amy didn't want a tabby and white cat. She wanted a black one. A very particular black one.

"Has Charlie finished his dinner, Sarah? Can we let Jet in?" Mrs. Jones was peering around the kitchen door, with Jet in her arms.

Charlie looked up at her and hissed angrily. He hadn't finished, and he didn't want that kitten anywhere near his food.

"Oh, Charlie," Sarah sighed. "They really aren't getting along any better, are they?"

Mrs. Jones shook her head. "I'm beginning to wonder if I did the right thing," she admitted, her voice sad. "Maybe I should have let that little girl keep her. You could see she was heartbroken when she brought Jet back."

"But you'd miss her!" Sarah protested.

"Of course I would! But I think she'd be well taken care of. And we still have Charlie. He's a wonderful boy, but he just doesn't like sharing his house...."

Sarah nodded. "Oh, he's finished." She picked up Charlie and took him over to the door to put him outside.

Misty watched as Sarah began to open the door, and her whiskers trembled with sudden excitement. The yard! The fence! And along the fence, just waiting for her, was Amy's yard, and Amy's house, and Amy.

She wriggled frantically and made the most enormous leap out of Mrs. Jones's arms. She shot out of the door before Sarah could even think to shut it.

She was going home.

Amy sighed, and stared down at her homework. She was supposed to be writing about her favorite place, but the only place she could think of was the tree house, with Misty curled up on the beanbag. A sudden scuffling at the kitchen window made her look up.

"Misty!" Dad exclaimed, looking up from the pan he was stirring on the stove.

Amy ran to the door to let her in. She knelt down and swept Misty up into her arms. Misty purred gleefully, rubbing her face against Amy's.

Amy was laughing and crying at the same time. "She came back," she muttered, and Misty licked her hand gently. Amy's dad tickled Misty under the chin, and then her mom came over to pet her, too.

"Mom, do we have to…?" Amy asked miserably. "She's so happy to be here…." She looked pleadingly over at her dad, but he shook his head sadly.

Her mom sighed. "I know. I wish we could just keep her, but it wouldn't be fair. She doesn't belong to us." She picked up the phone.

"Mrs. Jones? It's Emily Griffiths. Yes, I'm afraid we have Misty again. Sorry, I mean Jet."

Amy sat down on one of the kitchen chairs and petted Misty as she watched her mom miserably.

Her dad put a comforting hand on her shoulder. *Maybe Mrs. Jones was going out*, Amy thought. Maybe it wouldn't be a good time to bring Misty back, and they could keep her for just one night. But that would be worse, wouldn't it? She'd never be able to give her up then.

Misty wriggled indignantly as a tear fell on her head, and then another.

"Really?" The note of surprise in her mom's voice made Amy look up. "Well, if you're sure. We'd be delighted."

Amy stared at her, sudden hope making her feel almost sick. She watched her mother put down the phone and turn around, beaming. "That was the first time Misty had been out, Amy.

She came straight back to you. Mrs. Jones says that she obviously thinks she's your cat now, and it isn't fair to keep her. She's given Misty to you." She hugged them all—Amy and Misty and Dad together. "Well, we promised you a kitten, didn't we?"

"Oh, Mom! Wait a minute." Amy pressed Misty gently into her dad's arms and dashed upstairs, then raced back down again and into the kitchen with something pink in her hand.

Carefully, she fastened Misty's collar around the kitten's neck. "You're really ours now. You're here to stay," Amy muttered, taking the kitten from Dad.

Snuggling against Amy's neck, Misty closed her eyes and purred—a tiny, happy noise. She was home!

HOLLY WEBB

Holly Webb started out as a children's book editor, and wrote her first series for the publisher she worked for. She has been writing ever since, with more than 100 books to her name. Holly lives in England with her husband, three young sons, and several cats who are always nosing around when she is trying to type on her laptop.

For more information
about Holly Webb visit:

www.holly-webb.com
www.tigertalesbooks.com